2125 - The Hibernator

What if you wake up in 100 years?

Fons Burger

ISBN

© *Dif Books*

Difbooks is a part of Brighter World Dif Books B.V.

Cover design: Pieter Schol

Design: Yuri Jansen

Print: Zalsman, Zwolle

No part of this publication may be disclosed by print, photocopy, internet, e-reader or any other means without prior written permission from the publisher.

Also available as an e-book and audiobook read by Paul van Soest.

Contents

Foreword	1
Chapter 1	3
Chapter 2	47
Chapter 3	85
Chapter 4	113
Chapter 5	143
Epilogue	161
Afterword	163

FONS BURGER

This book is dedicated to my children, grandchildren and their descendants.

Chapter 1

A bitter acid sensation sets fire to his nose, mouth and throat. He thinks he is suffocating, gasps for air. It feels as if the oxygen he breathes in, flows straight to his brain. As if his windpipe is connected directly to the blood vessels in his grey matter. The burning pain mixes with the euphoric feeling that too much oxygen causes.

Something is moving above his head. His eyes are still closed, but there is so much light that he can perceive the outlines of that something. Max feels his mouth being pushed open by something soft, pressing into his jaw. Something solid is now attached to it, making a sucking, slurping sound. Another hard object, slightly thinner and pointier, enters between his teeth and a liquid suddenly squirts through his mouth. It feels deliciously fresh and has a taste he recognizes. He can't think of the word, realizes that almost no words come to mind. There is the image of a round white object, but he isn't sure if that is a projection, outside, above him, in front of his closed eyes, or if it is an indistinct thought floating around in his head.

There's a sound. Humming. Because he also feels something vibrating in his body, he realizes that he might be the one making that sound. He enjoys both the cooling liquid in his mouth and the vibrations felt somewhere halfway down his body.

At once it is dark in front of his eyes, an unpleasant shadow hanging over him. He hears bubbling and humming everywhere around him. It feels as if he is underwater and someone is trying to talk to him. But close to his ear he also hears a beep, a constant rhythm reverberating into the space around him. Then there is a violent, heavy clatter that he also vaguely recognizes. He searches again for the word that goes with it, tries to think of where he has heard it before.

Peppermint comes to mind, but no, that's the word he was looking for just before. The taste of peppermint. By now the rinsing in his mouth has stopped and the leftover fluid is being sucked out. The bitter taste returns slowly but weaker, softer, more bearable.

He now hears the sound coming from all sides. Just before he starts to slide back into the intensely black darkness he had come from, the word comes to him: Applause, the clatter he heard a moment ago, was applause.

Everything goes black again.

Later, when the light returns, he wonders how long he has been out. An almost familiar scent reaches him. He can smell! The beeping is still there, or there again, but the light shining through his eyelids is different. Less piercing, like the air he breathes, he needs more of that now. Where am I? he wants to ask. But when he tries, he finds that he can't. A sound does come out of his throat but it's no more than a soft, toneless gurgle. Many thoughts shoot through his head. He notices his breath hitching and he also feels something now, something at a distance, something that somehow also belongs to him.

An oppressive feeling. A moment later, he realizes that it's inside of him.

In my body, he thinks and tries to push the other thoughts away. He tries to think of what that body looks like. His head, the ears that hear a beeping, his mouth, which now has only a faint taste of bitter acid left in it.

That oppressive feeling must be his stomach. He can't feel his legs. Or his arms. But wait, his arm is now being picked up by the wrist and he feels something or someone squeezing it. Endless thoughts shoot through his head again. Why didn't he hear anyone come in just now? Why can't he open his eyes? Why can't he speak? Where's the feeling in his legs?

Damn, he tries to say, but the only thing coming out of his mouth is that faint gurgle.

...&...

The only way he can determine that he's in a room is by the light and shadows because everything is white but in different shades. He sees a large, bright frame, a window, it's daytime. It must be a hospital bed because there's a handle above his head to pull himself up. A lot is going on around him. Someone is sitting in a chair at the end of his bed, but it isn't a regular chair, there are hoses and cords leading to or from it, he has no idea what or who it is.

Someone else is sitting next to him. He recognizes the voice, it's familiar. It's probably his regular doctor or nurse because he constantly wants to know how he is doing, if he feels pain anywhere, what the effect is of the pills being fed to him.

And what he sees.

I can't see diddly-squat, he says, his voice still sounding hoarse but getting better the last few days.

Diddly what? asks the voice, what do you mean Max?

Max, he murmurs. Yes Max. I am Max.

Yes, Max Flowerday. Tell me what you see.

Everything is fuzzy, very fuzzy. Like I need glasses. Very strong ones. Do I have glasses?

He feels a vast tiredness overwhelm him, closes his eyes and sinks into the blackness. The last thing he hears is the man saying that all glasses, except sunglasses perhaps, are very old-fashioned.

He loves darkness and sleep. He dives into them and takes shelter there for as long as he can because when he is awake, everything takes effort. But if he dives in too deeply, all sorts of people come to him again, images, situations, events that mostly just confuse him. He knows the people, but he can't remember their names, or what they mean to him. A neighbor, a child, a parent, an acquaintance? He doesn't know. In his dream, though, he suddenly sees the man sitting at the end of his bed very clearly. He's a young man, looking sullen and busily swearing, complaining that all his blood is being sucked out of him. Then he feels somebody shaking him, the man still sitting next to him telling him he must stay awake.

It will take some time, he says, it's in your blood and glands but don't worry, it isn't very complicated these days, he hears him say.

Doesn't he remember having an illness? Wasn't it very bad? Bad as in hopeless? He hates that damn memory of his, it's a muddle and the harder he tries, the more all the thoughts blend together.

He forces himself to think, he needs clarity. So he's in a hospital, has a serious illness that suddenly isn't all that serious anymore. Someone is constantly at his bedside. And there's a grumbling young man by the foot of his bed, connected to him via hoses and cords.

Who is sitting there in that chair? he asks. That's Simon. Simon Flowerday, comes the reply.

Max remembers that surname. Yes, of course, he just heard it. That's his name, too.

A relative of mine?

The room remains silent for a while. A cough, a sigh, someone seems to be doing some serious thinking.

He's your grandchild or actually your great-great-grandchild. Okay, says Max. What's he doing there? Why is he grumbling so much? It's a bit complicated to explain all of that now, we're borrowing his blood to make yours better.

It's quite exhausting for him, takes a lot of energy.

Then the family relationship hits him.

Great-great-grandchild? He wonders for a moment. A grandchild is a child of your son or daughter. They then have a child and that is a great-grandchild, he recalls. But a great-great-grandchild? Four generations on?

I will explain that to you as well, Max.

That would make me very old.

Very old, Max.

…&…

The machine into which he must put his head makes him anxious; the liquid that is sprayed into his eyes hurts. A voice asks if he feels anything, and when Max curses, the voice says the anesthetic will take effect soon.

His eyelids are automatically caught in some kind of clamp and held open. He's instructed to keep his eyes still and to focus on a bright light that has sprung up in front of him. He sees a sharp object coming towards his eye and as it enters his frozen gaze, hears a slurping sound.

Then comes time for his other eye's procedure, which goes more smoothly because the anesthetic has had more time to take effect.

The robotic arms barely make a sound and in less than a minute he hears the voice say: ready!

Now he can sit up straight. He looks around, startled. The vague outlines he has so far observed from his bed, the table, chairs, the bunch of flowers and some fuzzy posters on the wall, are suddenly all razor-sharp. The view takes his breath away. Something is projected on the wall and the ophthalmologist asks Max to tell him which letters he sees. Max thinks. Letters, words, text, he isn't quite there yet. He sees the figures sharply, recognizes shapes, but can't name them.

Perhaps something has gone wrong. Can't you read anymore? the ophthalmologist asks kindly.

I don't know, says Max. All of this just doesn't mean anything to me right now.

The man shrugs.

I'll just test the projection, he says and presses a few buttons. Some icons suddenly flash on in Max's field of vision. They startle him, especially because when he turns his head, the icons remain in front of him, at the same spot, no matter which way he looks.

What the hell, he says angrily. There's something in my eyes, he exclaims. What have you done?

So what do you see?

A bunch of green figures, he says angrily.

Easy, easy, the ophthalmologist says hastily and presses a button. Now they're gone, aren't they? I'll deactivate this feature for now.

Without another word, the ophthalmologist drags the machine out behind him and leaves Max's room. Before the door can slam shut, someone pushes it open again, two men enter. Max is stunned; he now sees everything with razor-sharp clarity.

Well, Max, is this a good time? I hope it wasn't too bad? They inserted artlenti into your eyes. Your natural lenses have been replaced, so to speak, by better, multifunctional ones. You'll get used to them in a few days.

Max recognizes the voice. The man had introduced himself earlier as Doctor Jan Drent, his personal beacon amidst all this insanity. Standing next to Drent is a young man with dark skin, big green eyes and a tight jawline. He wears a white coat and something indefinable hangs around his neck.

Jan Drent, Max exclaims, I can see you! I can see you, man! What a miracle.

Jan smiles faintly. He points to the young man standing diagonally behind him. Curiously, this person looks vaguely familiar to Max.

So here he is, says Jan. Your great-great-grandson Simon. Simon this is Max, Max this is Simon.

Max smiles as kindly as he can, but he sees that it doesn't come across. Instinctively, he reaches out his hand to shake Simon's. Simon is startled, looks confused and puts his hand on his heart. He nods his head gently.

Oh, Max just says and waves his outstretched hand a little. He tries to stand up but only partially succeeds. He pulls his legs up and beckons Simon closer.

Simon, Max mutters. You're related to me? Ha ha, am I your grandfather, or your great-great-grandfather even?

Simon flinches a little because of the laugh that apparently sounds rather sinister. Max thinks he sees aversion in his eyes.

Understandable, since he looked at himself in the mirror this morning: his skin looks strange, his bald, wrinkled head resembles a giant, shriveled seed potato. There are two bags under his eyes, spacious enough to hold a pigeon egg.

Yes, good afternoon, Simon says politely. Are you feeling better yet? All three of them chuckle as they realize the triviality of the question.

Max doesn't answer. He's suddenly very tired and lets himself fall back against the sloping upper part of the bed. He looks intently at his two visitors. Has he seen this Simon before or does he look remarkably like someone he used to know? He has started dividing his memory into circles with a post in the middle. One post for people, one for the surroundings, one for events, one for facts and one for miscellaneous. Closer to the post, the memories are clearer than those at the edge of the circle. This Simon belonged in the family circle, close to the center. Does he resemble his son? Did he have a son?

I'm Max Flowerday, says Max. It's something of a mantra that he learned. Drent had said it to him over and over again after he had asked: Who am I?

You are Max Flowerday, Jan said then.

Since then, he has been saying it 20 times a day and he seems to be getting used to the name, although it might just be a name people have given him, he doesn't have a clue. But then Simon says: That's also my name, Flowerday, Simon Flowerday.

…&…

A girl in tight white overalls has just put a plate with a shiny, silver dish cover in front of him. Max sees himself in it, distorted as if in a funhouse mirror. Underneath it is his lunch, he knows.

In the past few days, he has been seeing images of a large piece of tender, Argentinian beef lying on a well-lit barbecue in his mind's eye. A beautiful, crispy, almost blackened exterior, the liquid sizzling out when poked with a fork. He can almost recall the flavor.

Don't you want to watch? the girl asks with a practiced smile. She is new to the ward, or he has been moved from another ward, he can't quite recall which. She wants to take the lid off his plate, but he grabs her by the arm.

The girl looks startled at the fingers around her wrist and pulls her arm back roughly.

Wait just a moment, says Max, I'm imagining there is an Argentine 'bife de lomo' underneath, fresh from the barbecue. He closes his eyes and feels his mouth start to water. When he opens his eyes again, he sees the puzzlement in the girl's eyes.

Don't tell me you don't know what beef is, says Max, adding almost pleadingly: please.

Hah, of course I know what beef is, she says, after recovering from his touch.

Max is relieved and asks if she can arrange a big steak for him one of these days.

A stake in what? she asks. Confusion suddenly reigns.

But after all misunderstandings are resolved with some giggles, she says that meat is not really on the menu in this hospital, or in any hospital for that matter. And meat coming from Argentina, well, she certainly never heard of such a thing.

A small piece of beef would cost as much as 100 creds, she adds. Way too expensive for me.

Max looks disappointed but also manages a shy laugh at his own expense. He has no idea how much 100 creds is but surely he would be willing to give it up for a bife de lomo.

After the girl removes the cover and leaves the room, Max sighs deeply again. He sees a cup of broth and a deep plate with mixed vegetables blended into a mush with some large mushrooms on top. There's also a small bowl with a yellowish kind of custard. He sips from the hot broth carefully. It has a strange taste and an even stranger smell, but by the second and third spoonful he swallows, he comes to appreciate the taste.

Looking at the tray, a vague memory of hospital food suddenly comes to him.

Foodwise, hospitals haven't improved much, I might even start longing back to the slop they used to serve in the old days, he grumbles.

There is no one in the room to hear his complaints.

A few minutes later, Doctor Drent is in his room. He greets him warmly with his hand on his chest and sits down on a chair next to Max's bed.

I hear you have complaints about the food, says Drent.

Max looks at him in surprise. He knows he hasn't complained to the kitchen girl, he did no more than joke about steak a bit.

You said hospital food hasn't improved much, Drent says to clarify.

Max looks around startled. Are they spying on him? His eyes scan the room. The small, round objects he noticed before in the ceiling corners, he now realizes what they are. Come to think of it, the mirror is also conspicuously integrated into the wall.

Normally, people sign our terms and conditions upon arrival, Drent says, but in your case that was a bit difficult, given the state you were in.

Drent smiles a little awkwardly and starts explaining that there really isn't anyone who's watching him all day.

What we do have are camera images and a computer that is constantly analyzing whether you're okay, whether you need something or, as happened now, make comments. Because we want to keep an extra close eye on things in your case, it's set to a rather high level of sensitivity. Drent smiles again, a bit sheepishly now.

There is a private mode though. All you have to do is ask for it, he says. Just say 'camera off'. That will turn the system off and no one will be able to see or hear you. It would be better if you don't do that too often because the program alerts us if you become unwell. Or if something interesting happens to which we have to react.

Like my complaining, Max mutters.

Your comment about the old days, says Drent. And what you said about the bife de homo. Ha ha, it sounds like you all used to eat human meat. What really matters to me is that obviously you're starting to remember things. Things that happened a hundred years or more ago. That's good news, Max.

Lomo, Max thinks, loins, indeed he realizes this is a memory. But then the number hits him.

A hundred years... he says hesitantly. And then he asks: a hundred years?

Yes Max, you spent a hundred years in a coma.

But that's impossible, Max exclaims. Right? That's impossible, isn't it? Say it's impossible.

Drent puts his hand on Max's arm. He looks at him intently, searching for words.

A hundred years ago, there was an experimental clinic in Mexico that put people in a coma and could stop the ageing process completely with dubious methods, Drent says. A kind of room-temperature cryonization. An extremely long hibernation.

Max's jaw drops, literally and figuratively, he sucks in air and holds his breath. He wonders if Drent is joking, even though he knows he is not.

I don't remember any of it, Max says.

So much is suddenly going on in his head. That he had been in a coma for a long time had dawned on him by now, but a hundred years? A century?

I was sick, says Max, I was sick, right? I was going to die anyway?

Yes Max, you were incurably ill.

Drent clicks his tongue and asks for a numbered file. The mirror built into the wall now suddenly shows a photo. Max sees himself, but not as before, when the mirror was still just a mirror, not the tired head with confused eyes and the sagging facial skin. It's a photo in which he is smiling broadly, with a big head of hair and a healthy colour in his smooth cheeks. At least, if he is indeed the man in that photo. Before he can speak, Drent clicks his tongue and a second photo appears on the screen. Max looks intently at the people in it. They are barefoot, the beach is bright white, the sky a clear blue. He sees two children, one a girl and one a boy who looks a bit like Simon. A grumpy man in the middle, that must be him. Next to him is a woman, his wife? Yes that must be his wife, a lot younger than him and beautiful, very beautiful, with curly hair, a proud look in her eyes and a broad smile around her lips.

That's Felice, Max says spontaneously. He doesn't really know where the name came from. It's just there all of a sudden.

Felice, yes, she's my wife. Is this a picture from a hundred years ago? And those children. Daan and Sam, he suddenly knows and he speaks their names aloud. Daan and Sam.

He dares not ask if they're all dead.

...&...

The nurse pushes him out of the hospital. In an old-fashioned wheelchair without a motor, joystick or any other modern additions. When they stop he gets up because he can walk on his own, he has trained his legs vigorously in recent weeks, as well as the rest of his muscles, carefully, one by one, group by group. Some hairs have tentatively returned to his head. The Plastic Tech department has already tightened the sagging skin around his head and body quite a bit. They've also tinkered with his brain. They bombarded his little grey cells with electric pulses on his skull, light and sound waves and endless exercises. He started remembering more and more over the past two months. His posts got higher, his circles bigger and what was in them became clearer.

It's like having reverse dementia, he had told Drent. In ordinary dementia, you first lose your short-term memory, then your long-term memory fades away until finally you can't remember the names of your own children anymore and you slowly sink into total oblivion before turning into a vegetable.

With me, it went the other way around. I woke up a vegetable, I seemed to have no past at all, but my memory gradually got better and better. In tiny steps, more and more memories from longer and longer ago returned, so now I even remember the names of my children and grandchildren again.

A vehicle slowly approaches the entrance of the hospital, it's a simple thing, just a basic frame on wheels with an open cabin with an open cabin at the back, covered by a small roof to provide shelter from the rain. The cabin has six seats.

It somehow reminds Max of a shuttle for the elderly at amusement parks or cheap airports, but with big wheels and poor design. It has no aerodynamic lines whatsoever, but they would serve no purpose anyway, given the vehicle's pathetic pace. Max notices that there is no one behind the wheel; indeed, there is no steering wheel. Aïcha, Simon's wife, sits in the back. He waves excitedly at her; she jumps out of the car before it has fully stopped. The vehicle seemingly objects to this and voices some safety concerns, but she runs towards him, wraps her arms around him and hugs him tightly.

Come here Max, give me a big hug, she exclaims. It's finally allowed, no more germophobic hospital patrol to stop us now.

Aïcha is half a head taller than he is and has a full mane of dark curls. Her bright blue eyes don't really match her olive skin and the North African features in her appearance.

Max looks up at her a little helplessly at first, then frees himself from her firm hold and wraps his arms around her. He feels the warmth of her body through the curious fabric of the suit she's wearing, her moist breath on his neck after she puts her chin on his shoulder, even the beating of her heart. A wonderful sensation, the best he's had since waking from his coma. He wants to say that he could stand there like that for another hundred years but reckons that such a remark might sound a bit odd coming from him.

The car didn't wait for them and went on its way to its next cargo. Max apologizes for holding her for so long, Aïcha shrugs her shoulders cheerfully. She presses her ear for a moment, Max sees one of those devices there, small and elegant. He had to get one as well, they had explained to him in the hospital, because that's how everyone communicates these days, and with those artlenti, those lenses that project annoying texts into the corners of his eyes.

Max had asked for a mobile phone, but everyone had laughed heartily at that.

Aïcha utters the word 'taxi' and another one is already approaching. It's an even uglier model in a fire-engine-red and with sliding doors that open automatically. They take a seat in the back and Aïcha mentions an address. The doors close and the vehicle starts moving.

He looks out of the window at the city where he last took a taxi to the airport a hundred years ago. Through the open window, he listens to the sounds of the city. He hears the whispering of wheels over the road surface that has a strange sheen. It's clearly not asphalt; he doesn't recognize it. A ship's horn in the distance. The rustling of trees and some laughter from people passing by on the pavement. Otherwise, it's pretty quiet.

It used to be crowded here all the time. Where have all those people gone? he asks. Aïcha watches silently.

There are still some houses from his time but there are many gaps in between the buildings, with gardens, parks and trees to fill the open spaces. The new houses are made of a material unknown to Max. Aïcha tells him what it's called, something with printing, but it doesn't mean anything to him. He also sees a lot of wood and glass, tall buildings with terraces up to the penthouses. Walkers, cyclists and more taxis calmly slide past each other. The air is clean, the sun shining brightly. The pace seems slower than it used to be, back in the day everything had to be done faster and faster all the time. In between the traffic, he sees the remains of what his city was once. Tall mansions, the odd church here and there, converted into apartment buildings with windows behind which he can see daily life. The iron gate, a work of art highlighting the spot where a city gate once stood, still looks well maintained.

As does the town hall they drive past, a squat building in beaux-arts-style with neo-Romanesque influences. He suddenly remembers standing on the pavement there after a simple wedding ceremony with Felice. He tries hard to remember how long ago that was. Married 130 years, that sounds bizarre.

They disappear into a tunnel and the interior light flashes on. And? What do you think? Aïcha wants to know.

Well, what can I say, Max replies, it all looks quite logical, though it's crazy that half the city has been demolished now, so much green. You used to have to look very hard to find a patch of grass, and when you found one, it was usually covered in dog shit. The gardens were all covered with toxic soil, so nothing much grew there. On the other hand, it doesn't look very modern, architecturally speaking. Quite a scrappy mess.

Aïcha smiles.

There has been a lot of innovation in architecture and urban development, she says, but then everything was reversed and after that, it went back and forth and then back again. But some kind of balance was achieved eventually.

When they exit the tunnel, they're almost immediately in front of a wood and glass building at least 20 storeys high. It's surrounded by a park and a wide river flows past behind it. The building rises up in steps, with balconies showing lots of greenery. No waving trees or orderly plants, but messy, balcony-sized allotments.

This is where you'll live for now, Aïcha says as the car comes to a halt. Until we find you something else.

...&...

Even before Max and Aïcha reach the front door, it's opened by Simon. He slaps his hand on his heart in greeting and takes a step back. Max takes three steps forward, embraces Simon and presses him firmly against him. Simon struggles for a moment.

Max enjoys the touch again, the embrace, the two bodies against each other, the warmth radiating between. It's over, all that coldness, with those doctors and nurses in their white overalls, their rubber gloves and surgical masks. When he lets go of Simon, his great-great-grandson sighs with relief.

Felice, Grandpa Max is here, Simon calls out.

Max's thoughts immediately start to stray. As if he forgot for a moment that his super-grandchild was named after his wife Felice. The photos that Drent showed him thawed part of his frozen memory. In every picture he saw the beauty of his wife, who exuded such warmth, the dark eyes that always told a special story. It had felt so familiar and she had seemed so close.

The children required more effort. He patiently looked at the few images that had apparently been preserved. A birthday, a holiday photo. It all remained distant, far away, buried by time.

Felice, come greet Grandpa Max, now! Simon shouts again.

After some moping about the Grandpa Max title, he had decided he could live with it. The grandpa-to-the-max. Maximum old. At least that way they could also be done with all that great-great-grand-business and the third, fourth, fifth generation conundrums. In fact, he really is their primal grandfather.

Simon calls out to Felice a few more times. Then he walks to her room, annoyed, and slides open the door, standing broadly in the opening.

Max has come up behind him and looks over his shoulder at the girl sitting in front of a projection on the wall. She also has a bunch of curls, but they are blonde. Her face resembles Simon's, she wears some kind of jumpsuit with an indistinct painting printed or embroidered upon it.

She pauses the image on the wall. Max sees a pair of frozen cartoon characters.

Watching a movie? asks Max. No, schoolwork, says Felice. Ha ha, I don't believe that.

I'm doing maths!

Ah, my favorite subject.

Really? she says in amazement.

Of course not.

They both laugh.

Simon shows him around. The flat is small but very cozy. Besides Felice's room, there's a master bedroom and Simon's study. There's an inflatable bed there for Max. The living room is more spacious, with a sofa, a dining table and an open kitchen. Not a single book in the whole house, Max notes.

Books? No, paper is hardly produced anymore, Simon says. At the toilet he explains that the synthetic toilet bowl has a built-in water spray. When toilet paper became redundant, there was little reason to produce paper.

Nothing special either, says Max, they already had those toilets a hundred years ago in Japan.

They sit at the table. Simon had been cooking while Aïcha got Max out of the hospital. There's a small steak on Max's plate. The others have an indeterminate object next to their ratatouille and sweet potato, it looks somewhat like a wrinkled, round parsnip.

You shouldn't have, says Max. I happen to know how much meat costs. They told me that at the hospital. Enjoy it, Simon mumbles as he stares at the steak on his guest's plate. Max carefully cuts off a slice with his knife and puts it in his mouth. He closes his eyes and chews the steak slowly, transferring it from one corner of his mouth to the other. Then he cuts off another slice and presents it to Felice on his fork.

Ughh, I don't like meat, says Felice.

Because of the poor little animals? asks Max.

What animals? she asks.

Well, you know, farm cows that never see daylight and chickens living in a pen the size of one and a half times their ass. Or has that changed as well?

Felice laughs at the word ass but then pulls a face as if she has absolutely no idea what he's talking about.

Meat doesn't come from a cow or a chicken. Meat comes from the factory. Max laughs. Yeah, kids used to think pizza grew on trees!

Pizzas don't grow on trees, Felice says defiantly, daddy makes them out of water and flour. And they're delicious with fresh tomato and mozzarella.

Aha, so mozzarella still exists, Max sighs. That comes from cows as well, you know, because it's made from cow's milk. Or buffalo milk, of course. Are there still buffaloes?

Duh, milk comes from the factory too, says Felice. Simon is fed up with the discussion.

Cows and buffaloes are kept in the wild, in the countryside, he says. They loosen the earth with their trampling and grazing and fertilise it with their faeces. Their milk is for their young. When they get old and die, don't think you'll get a tender steak out of them. Their buttocks are as tough as a rubber bicycle tyre. Max leans forward, shrugs his shoulders and looks glumly at the piece of cultured meat in front of him. It doesn't taste bad, really, but does it taste like meat? He doesn't actually know. Can a tongue that has been out of action for a hundred years still distinguish flavors? And the brain connected to that tongue, can it remember taste? The taste of steak?

Aïcha calls something to him. He has been sitting with his fork raised for at least half a minute and everyone is looking intently at the piece of meat dangling from it.

Oh sorry, Max says and sticks it in his mouth. He then cuts the remaining steak in half and slides one half onto Simon's plate without asking. Simon almost objects but then looks at the piece of cultured meat in front of him with a happy expression on his face.

Anyway, I think it's very well done, Max says to no one in particular, well done by that cultured cow.

...&...

It's hot in Simon's study. Max has already opened the window and thrown off all the sheets. In the faint glow of a nearly full moon, he stares at his naked body lying on a soft bamboo sheet. He is milky white, like real, fresh mozzarella or like a blank piece of paper, also gone out of fashion in these changed times. His sex lies listlessly in his groin, his thighs are skinny with far too little muscle left, he can count his ribs.

His brain is fully engaged and a deep frown wrinkles his forehead.

How did all this come about a hundred years ago? Why doesn't he know? Drent told him about the rare blood disease he suffered from. But why had they left him in a coma for a hundred years? Had it taken so long for them to find a cure? Drent had said nothing about that. But according to that same Drent, mankind had managed to cure the bulk of other diseases like cancer, diabetes, Alzheimer's a long time ago.

He drifts away for a while.

There's Felice, no, not the little Felice. This is his Felice, the Felice from the picture. The Felice who is his wife. Or was. And now she's gone again. No, there she is again. She's very close, he can almost touch her olive skin, trace the curve of her face with his fingertips. She shows him what she has just put on. Long black wide-leg trousers, a beautiful cashmere pullover and high heels, very high heels. As always, he has to approve her clothes for the day. He knows 'very unusual' is the wrong thing to say, because she'll immediately go and change. Or: 'Gee, where did you buy that?', also wrong, out it goes. That's why he always says she looks great because she usually does.

He wants to talk to her, there are a million things he would like to ask and say, but she's busy tidying the bedroom, collecting the dirty laundry, rolling up her yoga mat, putting away a singing bowl. She asks if he wants breakfast. Breakfast? It's the middle of the night, he thinks. Let's go to bed, I'll undress you carefully and put your clothes on your chair, neatly folded. And then I'll crawl next to you to enjoy the warmth of your skin. We will sleep, sleep soundly.

He jerks awake or was he already awake? Is it much later? Or has he been gone less than a minute? His eyes scan the room for a clock.

He tries to hear if any birds are chirping yet, in the hospital he used them to determine how the morning was progressing. He thinks of Felice, his Felice, who was here just now showing off her clothes. How could he have left her? Had she left him? Had she still been alive? He closes his eyes and tries to see her again. But she's gone. The bedroom where she wandered around a moment ago is empty. The light is off, nothing stirs, there is nothing but darkness. Until he drifts off again.

Daan is holding his hand. Daan, his son, he recognizes him instantly, as if he had seen him just yesterday, so clearly.

Daan sweeps back his blonde hair, and his tear-stained eyes become visible. He keeps cursing. Out loud and ever louder, but he's also crying. Max tries to comfort him, he doesn't know what to say, he has a huge lump in his throat.

He realizes he is somewhere unfamiliar. A white, hospital-like room, overlooking a desert. He sees the heat shimmering over a vast expanse of sand. An unimaginable emptiness with nothing more than some stray bushes or cacti. There is a bed in the room and a tube connects him to an inverted bottle from which a liquid slowly drips.

He wants to cry but he feels a deep sleep coming on. He wants to say something to Daan but his mouth refuses to cooperate.

When he finds himself back in Simon's room again, all his ribs convulsing, he sits upright in bed. Was that how it ended a hundred years ago? When he opens his eyes, the tears that have gathered behind his eyelids stream down his cheeks.

Felice is back and comforts him.

Max wants to say something to her, but she has already disappeared again.

...&...

The river still meanders right through his city, its banks connected by rails and bridges. He looks out over the water and tries to recall the skyline as it was a hundred years ago. Many of the skyscrapers from back then are still standing. Like the four-star hotel where he liked to have lunch on the 43rd floor with fellow professors, before returning to the university slightly inebriated to give another lecture. The courthouse where he regularly had to appear at trials as an expert witness. A large theatre where he once gave a Ted Talk. But it's as if the tall buildings tower like tombstones over a beautiful, tangled world of wooden buildings no higher than three or four storeys, surrounded by trees, shrubs, flowerbeds and parks. Only a high quayside wall draws a grey line under the beautiful, green chaos that seems to have settled on the other side of the river.

A man standing next to him throws bread from a paper-looking bag into the water sloshing against the quay wall below them. Gulls, ducks, crows, sparrows, swans, Max says to himself. And what are those birds?

Which ones? Which ones? the man asks eagerly. He is either in need of a chat or an avid birder, Max thinks and wants to walk on. The man is wearing a neat, long woolen or cashmere coat, but on his feet he has a pair of tired white trainers, worn out, muddy. Max briefly checks to see if he can point out the unknown bird species, but there are too many. He shrugs his shoulders.

The man looks at Max with some suspicion.

I've been away for a while, says Max. A lot has changed around here. He points to the other side. The man looks across and then back at Max.

So where did you do time? he asks with one eyebrow raised and the other as far down as possible.

2125 - THE HIBERNATOR

No, no I didn't do time, I was in a coma for a while, a very long while, Max replies.

It remains silent for a while.

The man looks ahead, shrugs and throws the last scraps of bread from the bag at the twittering birds. Fancy a cup of coffee over there? he asks Max as he points to a small pavilion, built on top of the quay wall a little further on.

Sounds great, says Max. I don't have any money with me though, so I'd love one but only if you're buying.

Money? mutters the man, you mean those dirty paper notes that everyone used to touch with their grubby paws? Ha ha, or one of those wallets full of useless metal? No, that was abolished some time ago. Money meant crime, smuggling, murder, drugs, all cash in hand. Black money, an entire black economy even. People evaded taxes, worked illegally, you could have someone killed for a pile of paper. Now you can't hide your money anymore, haha, it's all here. His flat hand indicates the inside of his wrist.

Max has already understood that you have to pay with a chip these days. He will get one soon, but nobody told him that it's implanted on the inside of your wrist. He peers at the man's wrist to see if he notices anything, but he doesn't. Then he shrugs.

As long as he pays for my coffee, he thinks.

...&...

His old house is still standing, the strip of grass it always overlooked also still exists but has changed beyond recognition. The long, boring lawns and straight town canal have given way to a tangle of paths, ponds, pieces of woodland with trees, bushes and a huge variety of other vegetation. Spring is already well underway and many things are in bloom. There are several spots with small glass domes, also filled to the brim with all kinds of plants. Somewhere halfway, a huge winter garden towers above the trees.

Max finds a bench overlooking his erstwhile home, a stately building constructed in 1900 to serve as an oversized single-family home for a shipping magnate. In World War II, it was home to the Sicherheitsdienst, which tortured and executed resistance fighters in the basement. Had he been superstitious, he would never have moved there because of all the tormented souls whose death cries might still be reverberating from the walls.

He thinks of his own soul.

Maybe it hasn't returned to my body yet, he thinks, or is still in a coma. They are scientifically capable of keeping me asleep for a hundred years. My liver, intestines and adrenal glands can purify blood again, digest food and produce hormones. My body, an intricate machine, with thousands of coordinated functions, the chemistry of bacteria, brain matter, proteins, molecules, atoms, quarks, billions of cells strung together with unique DNA strands, you might be able to shut it down, pause it for a hundred years, then reboot it again, barely older. In fact, my brain is starting to work even better now.

But my soul? thinks Max, that's a totally different story

There's a lot of coming and going at the building. Apparently, many more people live there now than when he lived there with Felice.

He closes his eyes.

Felice greets him. She sits behind her laptop in their ground-floor office and is happy to see him. A white mini bull terrier with a big black spot around his left eye jumps up to him. His name is Mascot. He feels his favorite animal's coarse nails through the fabric of his trousers. He asks Felice if she's finished working yet and what she would like to eat. There are numerous workstations for her employees in the large office space, but apparently everyone has already left for the day.

He climbs a staircase and enters the living room, a large, open space with a sitting area, a huge countertop, a kitchen island and a black grand piano. Then he starts pacing in front of the window. He reviews his day, the troublesome students, the difficult lecture, the clashes with his colleagues, that discussion at the golf club bar. He processes it all while walking, back and forth, overlooking the city. It's his moment to meditate, his way to unwind, to still his head. Back and forth, with maddening relentlessness, like a polar bear in a cage. That's the pet name Felice had given him: the Polar Bear. But occasionally it drove her crazy.

Surrounding him are the things he loves. A ten-by-ten feet-picture he painted with his children to cover a mouldy spot on the wall. A lounge sofa with a huge TV screen. A dining table ten feet long, at which he regularly serves meals to his family and friends. His kitchen with his favorite steel pans and that one well-sharpened kitchen knife which he uses for everything; from cutting all ingredients to stirring in his pans with the handle.

He sits down behind the piano and starts playing. He sings too, in a raw, low whiskey voice, the song of a famous Italian lawyer. This is how he always lures Felice upstairs.

After a while, she will come and sit next to him on the piano stool. She puts her arm around him. She loves it when he lets loose on the keys, especially when he sings along with it.

Are you okay there, sir?

2125 - THE HIBERNATOR

With a jolt, Max is back in the park. He wants to snap at the person dragging him out of his daydream but looks into the disarming face of a girl about 25 years old. She's conspicuously dressed in a bright purple satin-like dress, covered in all sorts of curved metal bits and tiny mirrors, and a pair of high white patent leather boots. Her face shows traces of Asian, Latin American and Northern blood. A perfect blend of perhaps four or five continents. She has long, dark hair, but her eyes are bright blue.

You were making a strange noise, she says. And your eyes were closed. I was singing, Max says. In my mind, anyway. Seeing that the young woman looks at him as if she's dealing with a disturbed person, he adds that he was daydreaming a little.

About the old days. I used to live in that house over there, at number 219. That was a long time ago, though. I had a piano, a big grand piano, and I would sit behind it to play and sing.

It's nice to be able to make music, she says and introduces herself.

My name is Antoine Verdaan, I live at number 192. Are you a musician? Oh no, says Max. I only play for fun. I am, I was, and he falls silent for a moment. I am a historian, I wrote and taught at the university. Antoine understands. This old man has a memory problem.

If you need help, I can walk you home, she says. Max looks at her with annoyance.

No, I'm not demented yet, young lady. I do remember where I live. But you see, you never stop being a historian or a professor. Being a writer or a teacher isn't like that, so I did indeed stop doing that a hundred years ago.

Antoine smiles with a little suspicion in her eyes.

Yes, I'm sure it was a while ago. History is no longer a university subject, and history lessons are no longer taught at school either.

What the hell? sighs Max. What do you mean: no longer taught?

Just that history classes have all been cancelled.

That can't be right. Then how are people supposed to know what happened in the past, the last few centuries, millennia?

Well, says Antoine, I'd better ask you that. I wasn't born yet, you know, when they were cancelled. I'm studying humanities.

Hmm, which one?

What do you mean?

Well, pedagogy, sociology, psychology, or some other -ogy? Phew, those are really ancient terms. Nowadays, everything is approached holistically. So, all those things you mentioned, as well as other things such as mental well-being, finance, spirituality, health, all those human aspects.

Sounds like a fairly unfocused department, Max mutters, like a sum total of medicine, economics, philosophy, theology and any number of humanities?

You seem a bit outdated, if I may say so, sir.

Max smiles. He holds out his hand and introduces himself.

Max Flowerday, nice to meet you.

Antoine looks a little perplexed at the outstretched hand, then puts her hand on her heart and takes a slight bow.

Max Flowerday, she says, that's a familiar name, or it used to be a long time ago anyway, a relation of yours? Wasn't he a professor?

Aha, so you do know something about the past, about history. You're just messing with me. No more history. It has a different name now, of course. Ancient sciences? What-happened-ology? He laughs a little sourly at his own joke.

Antoine looks at him with some pity again, as she did earlier. But she also seems confused. Max has no intention of telling her the story of his comatose past.

But was he related to you? Antoine asks again. They may have gotten rid of history as a subject, but that doesn't mean you can't be interested in the past.

Well, kind of related, you could say, he answers. What do you know about him?

Not much, she says, he was quite the pessimist, a cynic. Wrote a lot about the end of times. He was called the Doomsday Professor.

Max sees himself in one of the mirrors on her dress and is a little startled by his outward appearance. And of the description that he recalls vaguely. Doomsday Professor sounds pretty gloomy, it suits him.

Hmm, he says then, and what happened to him?

As far as I know it's quite a mystery. Suddenly he was gone, just like his wife, disappeared.

Max flinches.

His wife disappeared? he asks worriedly.

Yes, she was very famous, Felice Ricci, that disappearance was quite something.

Max feels a stab in his gut. Feelings of anger, helplessness, uncertainty and sadness overwhelm him, all at once. Why had no one told him?

The world seems to spin around him and he has to take a deep breath to stop it. Had Felice disappeared? How could he have forgotten that?

Disappeared. Gone from his life. Had he been looking for her? What had happened? He stands up and, after throwing Antoine a hasty goodbye, walks away at a brisk pace.

I didn't mean to offend your family Mr Flowerday, Antoine calls after him.

...&...

Good to see you healthy and well sir, says the woman opposite him. She kindly escorted Max from the front desk to her office and made some comments about the weather, which she thinks is still a bit chilly for the time of year. The sun shines through the windows of the wooden office building but disappears behind a cloud a moment later and doesn't show its face again. It suddenly makes the bright building look a lot gloomier, greyer, duller.

The local government official saved her speech for the privacy of her small office on the third floor of the town hall. Once there, she rattles on and on. Max has trouble following her. She talks about the quantum computing age, the basic income that has existed since 2064, the blockchain technology used by the Global Union of Mankind, the GUM, the world government. Max keeps nodding politely, staring out of the window at the garden her office overlooks. There is someone on his knees tending to the plants.

Distantly, he hears that since the introduction of the basic income, 61 years ago, he has received an income and therefore he's now incredibly wealthy.

Are you still following me?

Incredibly wealthy yes, Max says absently. It all means nothing to him.

The woman looks annoyed.

And what am I supposed to do in return? asks Max. I'm a historian, where can I apply for a job?

Well, that's problematic. Your profession has become obsolete. But you can retrain of course. Or make yourself useful to society in other ways.

Is there a helpdesk for that?

No, you have to figure that out for yourself with your guide.

Max has no idea which guide she's talking about, but he doesn't want to ask further. He wants to leave.

The woman leads him to another department. They pass a waiting room in which a dozen girls and boys are sitting. They all look up in surprise, as if they don't understand what Max is doing here. Behind the waiting room is a slightly older boy in a white coat, waiting for him. He has a gun in his hand and is waving it around like a cowboy.

You are the first person over 12 to come here for a wallet, he says cheerfully.

What are you going to do? Max asks, but instead of an answer, he gets the gun placed against his wrist, hears a click and feels a jab of pain in his wrist.

Damn, what the hell? shouts Max indignantly.

Your wallet, a chip, a miniscule-identity chip under your skin, says the boy. Your data is now in your wrist. He grabs Max's arm and pushes a cotton ball onto the bleeding puncture wound visible there. He sprays an adhesive plaster over it. He points to a screen that flashes on and says: Wallet of Max Milan Flowerday. He lists a long string of numbers. Instantly the screen changes and the boy points to it.

Wow, he says, looking at Max's account balance. I've never seen such a high amount. But then, judging by your date of birth, you're ancient, ha-ha. Seemingly unruffled, he continues with the formalities. Just a quick photo, fingerprints, iris and facial scan and your file is complete.

Hmm, says Max and tries to smile a little when he has to look at a lens that appears to be behind a computer screen. Then his hands are pushed into some kind of sandwich device, which registers his fingerprints.

After his visit to the town hall, he walks through the city. He can finally take a taxi now, but he still prefers to walk. The changes to the roads, streets and town canals remain fascinating. A chaotic collection of old houses, in clusters of no more than two or three, with beautiful works of art occasionally more than 30 feet high on the blind walls. Blocks where thousands of people used to live clustered together have turned into green fields with small houses widely spaced apart. Fields with vegetables, fruit bushes and trees are everywhere. Small parks with gazebos, bandstands and ponds. But also huge numbers of statues, carved from marble or some other kind of stone, baked out of clay or some other material and with colorful glazes, cast in bronze, almost as if everyone in the city has become a sculptor. He sees people strolling through the streets everywhere as if no one has to work.

He walks to the river, towards Aïcha's house and stops at the small café where he had coffee with the Bird Man. The girl behind the counter recognizes him and he orders a selection of her homemade baked goods. He also orders a glass of spirits to go with it, points to a bottle that has a large 45% printed on it, a double, on ice.

Then he sits down in front of the window and stares out without really seeing anything. He gulps down the drink, likes the taste but can't place it. He rattles the ice around the empty glass for a bit.

Then suddenly Felice is sitting opposite him. She puts her hand on his, he looks at it in amazement. Her hand is warm. He wants to say something to her, looks around nervously at first, no one there except the girl behind the counter. He doesn't want to come across as a confused old man, but he does want Felice to hear him, to know that he sees her.

That's why he whispers: where did you just come from?

Then she's gone. He bites his lip. Should he have kept his mouth shut? He brings his hand to his face, sniffs it and smells her. Her scent triggers a stream of random memories, as if he is leafing through a photo album in his head. His heart beats rapidly in his throat. He suddenly feels an intense chill go down his spine, searches for a word for the feeling that is overpowering him. Loneliness comes to mind, shit, he feels terribly lonely. Now he suddenly remembers the utter loneliness he felt after his Felice disappeared.

In his mind, he sees the photo he walked around with those final years, the portrait that was also on the back cover of her book. She gazes at the camera with something of a Mona-Lisa smile, but the look in her eyes is less sheepish than Mona's. She looked a little shy with that mysterious smile of hers. It's the picture he used when he couldn't sleep, the one he showed to others during his attempts to track her down, the one he kept sharing everywhere to keep her alive.

A tear slips down his cheek and travels to the corner of his mouth. He wipes it away before the girl can see him crying. Her baking is still untouched as he leaves the cafe again.

...&...

Mr Flowerday, he hears behind him. He's walking through the park in front of his former house again. The memories might come back more easily here. His 'Id' may have taken root here somewhere a hundred years ago or hid itself among the trees or bushes. The surroundings are familiar and yet at the same time they aren't.

Do you remember me? Antoine is standing right behind him. She's now wearing a strange white leather motorcycle suit, which probably won't be leather, but something very similar and factory-made. Antoine looks delighted. Max greets her hastily and wants to walk on but she cuts him off.

I know, she says.

What do you know?

I know who you are, she says.

Yes, of course Antoine and I also know who you are. You are Antoine Verdaan.

Yes, but you are Max Flowerday, THE Max Flowerday. Max looks puzzled. He sits down on the nearest bench, taps the seat with his hand.

Antoine sits down at a suitable distance, she watches him admiringly.

Tell me what you think, Max says.

I started sleuthing on The Net and found the story behind Max Flowerday.

Aha, you delved into history. I thought that was illegal, says Max.

Oh no, not illegal. Just hard to find for the average person. Antoine doesn't wait for Max to answer but continues without a pause. In 2025, you went to Mexico, where you asked an experimental clinic to put you into a coma.

You were married to Felice Ricci, the famous physicist and activist, discoverer of FreeEnergy salifusion, nominated for the Nobel Prize. She was kidnapped or went missing at least and never came back. In a way, you followed her. Disappeared as well.

That's quite a story, says Max. And you believe that this guy Flowerday just woke up again and is now sitting next to you?

Antoine's face shows disappointment as well as doubt, but then she pulls a screen, folded into quarters, out of her inside pocket. Clicks with her front teeth and says 'open'. A picture of Max from more than a hundred years ago appears.

So this isn't you? Max sees a healthy face with a good head of hair. He has a slightly arrogant look and a faint smile in the picture.

If that's me, I don't look much like myself, Max says and chuckles. You or he travelled to Ciudad Juárez. At the time, there was a clinic there where someone was experimenting with life-prolonging drugs. One of the experiments was called 'Coma Superviviente'. A coma that stopped the ageing process. Extremely controversial, by the way, even back then.

Antoine looks proud.

Max sighs.

I don't remember much of it, Max says now.

But it's true then, says Antoine almost jubilantly.

Hm, Max mutters. Yes, you're sitting next to a very old man.

You wrote about that experiment extensively at the time. I read a most enthusiastic essay published in an international journal. Coma Superviviente, the survivors' coma. You described it as something close to suicide, but the idea of waking up after a century or so and seeing what the world would be like then intrigued you greatly.

Only to find out now that history has more or less been erased, that the past no longer interests anyone, Max says cynically.

Well, *I* care, says Antoine.

Max sighs. You'd better introduce me to The Net. I'd like to know more about the past hundred years.

...&...

Max looks out across the river from the balcony. The ships navigating across it are moving slowly. Little Felice tried to explain to him how boats can move without fuel by using the force of the current, even going upstream. Max's brain automatically switches to 'stand-by' during such technical explanations. Felice also explained to him the workings of the little device behind his ear, which is connected, always and everywhere, to The Net and to his lenses, allowing him to read text messages and even see images. Still much to the dismay of Max, who keeps shouting that he has a speck of dirt in his eye, or rather a great many of them.

Seven o'clock, the sun is setting to the left of the river, and slowly sinks behind the skyline of what he dubbed the tombstones and in between the chaotic greenery and lower structures. He thinks of science fiction films from the old days. Around this year, all sorts of low-flying vehicles should have been zooming through the sky, in between gigantic towers with platforms. Huge screens everywhere with compelling messages from world leaders. Streets filled with drones and robots that either serve humanity and justice or have taken over completely.

What Max sees are walkers, cyclists and occasionally the self-driving cars which, in his opinion, are hideous. The only flying things are birds, quite a lot more than in his time.

Aïcha sits down next to him and hands him a cup of coffee.

Aïcha? he asks, can you explain to me why nobody wants to know about history anymore? Are the things that happened in the last century that horrible? And if so, whatever it was, it's already in the past, isn't it? Couldn't we learn from it?

A long silence ensues. A silence that the outside world only adds to. The boats on the river are quiet as a whisper, what little traffic there is only lets out a soft murmur of tyres, the birds have already retired for the night and from their nests, their chirping slowly subsides, little children everywhere have gone to bed. The magic hour casts a beautiful red glow over the world. A dog barks and they hear fragments of music coming from one of the neighbors.

It's hard to explain, says Aïcha. Especially to a historian like you. She takes a deep breath. Things have happened in the past hundred years that we would rather not be reminded of. Somewhere along the line, people decided not to bother with the past anymore. In the first decades of the last century, everything had become one big data tsunami. It was the time when states constantly rewrote their histories, where heroes became criminals and vice versa, where the truth hardly existed anymore, everything became subjective, alternative facts were made up, the media could no longer be trusted, science was vilified, journalists were mocked and persecuted.

She pauses for a moment, looks at Max who is listening to her intently. He says nothing, too afraid of losing his concentration. He wants to know and remember this.

One of the main things that contributed to that, she says, is the great DataFade. You have to remember that after we stopped using paper, eventually books weren't kept anymore either. During the war, they were used to light the stoves. Eventually, everything was stored digitally, all the information in big data centers. Well, imagine what happens when, in a war, all that data, operating programs, research, patents, literature... Aïcha stammers for a moment, trying to think of more examples. If all that is wiped out in one go after a major cyber-attack, the whole world comes to a standstill. But some people said: this is the time to start again, let's see this disaster as an opportunity for us to start over. Unencumbered by the past. Just bury it. Reconstructing history was the least important thing at that time. In fact, everyone was happy to have that source of countless conflicts erased. It felt like starting with a clean slate.

When the Global Union of Mankind was formed, the Peoples' Union, the decision was made to look at the present first and foremost. And to the future, and not just a few years or decades ahead, no, we wanted to start thinking in centuries or millennia out of a kind of respect for life, for the earth. There are still many survivors from the times before, but most of them are glad they no longer have to commemorate the victims of the terrible wars and disasters.

We have put that behind us, Max. We are only looking ahead now. It's more important to know where you are going than to know where you came from.

2125 - THE HIBERNATOR

Max wants to protest, but Aïcha puts a finger on her lips.

She's right, he needs to think about this. He can hear the cogs in his brain turning, or maybe it's the sound of his body cringing. In his old life, history meant everything to him.

And the more he begins to remember, the greater the need for knowledge, knowledge about the time he was away, knowledge about what has happened in the past hundred years. Can they really be uninterested in that? What's a country, a people, a world without history? he thinks. History is the sum of our existence. Who can understand anything about architecture, about technology, about human morality, if we don't know what others have thought or written about those things in the past, or what they invented? What mistakes have been made? How can we prevent wars? How can we say: never again? How can we understand human nature? Appreciate great inventions? How can we understand who we are, where we came from, where we need to go? Max thinks.

I get it, is all he says.

Aïcha bends forward and puts her hand with that olive skin on Max's forearm. She looks at him with her soft eyes.

History has brought us nothing good, she says. We always thought that humanity could learn something from history, but unfortunately it has never worked like that.

In Max's head a cacophony of voices is shouting: yes, but... With great effort, he manages not to say anything and with even more effort he quiets those voices. The silence that has fallen lasts until Simon cheerfully comes out onto the terrace with a couple of glasses of wine.

He has good news. A flat will soon become available two floors below them.

Perfect for you Max, he says, raising his glass in the air.

...&...

The door locks behind him. The electric mechanism makes a final clicking sound, but then there's silence. He takes a deep breath and inhales the scent of his new surroundings. It smells fresh but that's probably just the smell of the cleaning products used to wipe away all traces of the previous occupant's scents.

The flat is on the park side; it doesn't offer a harbor view like Aïcha and Simon's. Max overlooks a sea of greenery, also quite nice.

There are around a hundred flats in this building. The plinth houses shops and community spaces, a laundry, gym, studios and workshops.

Everyone knows each other.

Except for Max. Nobody knows him, except his family two floors up. He doesn't really know anyone else either. On his way out or in, everyone greets him with what he considers a vastly exaggerated friendliness. Even outside on the street, everyone is friendly. The whole world is full of friendliness. Quite irritating, Max thinks, quite unreal as well, as if he's an extra in a film about someone else's life.

This is the first time he's been really alone, a sensation he feels in his stomach. In the hospital, the door could open at any moment for a visit from the doctor, the nurse or someone from housekeeping. The cameras were watching him day and night; he never quite believed he could really turn them off. At Simon and Aïcha's house, he was never really alone either. Even when Simon took Felice to school, he would sit and wait for the door to open again. There are also thousands of cameras on the streets and in the park, clearly identifiable by those vicious red dots, lights indicating they are watching.

These cameras are apparently connected to a central computer that constantly records all movements outside and evaluates them with an algorithm. They recognize accidents, theft and violence and notify the emergency services immediately in case of danger.

Aïcha did not know the book 1984, did not know who Big Brother was, had never heard of George Orwell. When Max told her about the old days, about the time when privacy was highly valued, miscommunication erupted. So privacy was something you needed in order to do things you didn't want others to see, Aïcha concluded. Like what? she wanted to know.

Well, lack of privacy meant everyone could hear what you had to say, thought, did, Max said.

None of the street cameras turned out to have microphones. Max had to admit, of course, that it was nice that crime, murder and theft were curbed these days.

If everything about you is known and tracked in computer systems, he argued, you run the risk of being constantly harassed by salesmen trying to sell you something. That was already a problem back in his days, so it had to be completely outrageous now.

No, no, companies and individuals can't access that information, Aïcha told him.

What about sex then, intimacy, does that still exist with all these cameras? he tried.

That happens at home, Aïcha said, and there are no cameras there. Or you turn them off when your boyfriend or girlfriend comes over. Privacy is in your head, Max. And you can do anything you want at home. Outside, only crimes and accidents are reported, and who could object to that?

2125 - THE HIBERNATOR

He doesn't really know what to do now that he's finally alone. He could take off all his clothes, scream loudly, jump up and down on the bed, but just the thought that he could do all that is enough in itself. He sets out a course for something he hasn't done in a while: pacing. Along the balcony window, that's the longest route to walk back and forth and that will also allow him to look out. Walking from the window to the kitchen is also an option.

It's great. The Polar Bear walks back and forth. Getting rid of all the tension he had built up to dare enter this place.

When he stops pacing, Max goes to the kitchen, where he puts his hands on the kitchen counter. One by one, he opens the kitchen cupboards. Everything is made of wood, the whole building, even the walls, he notices when he taps them. The walls and ceilings consist of planks pushed together and there's a shiny and seamless parquet floor on the ground. If the previous occupant hadn't painted almost everything white, it would have looked like he was living in a tree house.

He only has four pieces of furniture so far for the three rooms in the flat. The study has a desk with a chair. The desktop consists of the usual screen glass that you can talk to but that's also touch-operated. Like his earpiece and lenses: everything, down to the light switches, oven and fridge, is connected to The Net. Max imagines a huge machine with enough brainpower to serve everyone and enable communication between people but sufficiently protected to prevent what happened in the past with the big DataFade. Perhaps there are also millions of tiny devices hidden everywhere in the walls of houses and buildings and connected to a super quantum brain.

His bedroom is occupied by a double bed. The few clothes he owns are piled up in the corner. The living room contains nothing but the easy chair he chose with Aïcha's help. She tried to convince him to get more furniture, but these were the only items he could decide on. The chair looks out of place standing in front of the window, looking out onto a balcony where the previous occupant left trays of dead plants and vegetables.

He sits down on the chair and opens the window. A fresh spring breeze flows into the room and fills his lungs. He hears children playing, dogs barking and the faint murmur of traffic. He enjoys the silence. This is better than Simon's music, which was always on way too loud. It's like a filtered silence, as all sounds are carried away by the wind between the park and the high apartment building, where he sits on the 14th floor. The wind is quite strong and shushes around his ears. Dusk sets in but he can't see the setting sun, his balcony faces east.

Then Felice enters.

She walks around the flat a bit dazed and talks loudly. Max stiffens.

But Max, you can't be serious about this, she shouts. It's like living in a coffin. A spacious one, true. But really, is that all you could find, just one chair, and an old-fashioned one that looks like crap at that. It must be comfortable, right? That's the only thing you judge a chair on. Just like your clothes when we first met. My god, always the same trousers and the same shirt, from the same shop, because they kept a card for you there with your sizes on it, so you never had to go near a fitting room, where the same girl always packed everything up for you without nagging.

Ha ha, and what about those socks you once won a hundred pairs of, because you had come up with a slogan for some beer brand; hideous socks, white with a red logo embroidered on them. Ah, yes, I get it. I always got to decide on everything, except our bed, your chairs and your desk, your opinions on those were so set that even I, with my good taste, didn't stand a chance.

Max wants to interrupt her, get up, say something, see if he can touch her. But he seems to be completely paralyzed. Yet he's sure he's awake, not dreaming.

Felice gesticulates wildly around the room, describing meticulously how he should decorate his flat. A drinks cabinet here, a sofa there. Down to the colour of the bookcase, the doors to hide his mess behind, the carpet pile height and the corner that would be most suitable for a piano.

Then she stands in front of him. She has tears in her eyes. She bends forward, he feels her breath, he really feels the warm air in his eyes, along his cheeks.

I miss you so much, Max says.

...&...

It's getting dark and Max figures he needs to do something about the lighting in his flat. Some lamps are hanging from the ceiling, but they give off a white, boring light that is far too bright. Felice apparently overlooked that, so she had to come back for a lighting plan. The glass screen built into the wall is the only other light source.

He pours himself a glass of spirits; it tastes like something fruity. He hasn't found his favorite drink yet. Most of the unfamiliar brands in his drinks cabinet do get him tipsy darn fast though. It's quiet around him and chilly because the window is open. He is too tired to get up and close it.

Aïcha gave him instructions on how to find his guide. All he had to do was sit in front of his desk and shout the command 'open', followed by his name.

A deep male voice emerges from the wall, politely announcing that he is Max's guide and asking Max to choose a name for him. Max has to think for a moment.

Ilse, he calls out. Ilse, that was the first search engine in my time. The male voice turns into a slightly older, upper-class female voice, cool and businesslike.

How can I be of assistance, Mr Flowerday? she asks.

Gee, you do sound a bit formal, Max lets slip. Sorry, how's this, Max?

Max looks surprised at the screen, where a woman now appears who looks nothing like an avatar. More like a flesh-and-blood human being, her voice is warm and informal.

You can still change some things about my appearance, says Ilse. Different hair, different clothes, different face, figure.

You're not real? I mean: not a real flesh-and-blood human being?

No, of course not, I'm a guide. Do you want me to change anything about my appearance?

No, no, you're fine like this, Max says a little shyly. Ilse has long ash-blonde hair, she looks slightly younger than Max and has a pretty face and a nice figure. He doesn't like the dress she's wearing but he wouldn't dare say anything about that.

What are you looking for? asks Ilse.

I'm looking for the past. History, that's what I'm looking for. What happened in the last hundred years?

That's a not very specific question.

Perhaps a review with the major events since... let's say, since 2025?

No, unfortunately I don't have that for you.

Books?

I have about 3 million of them in my library, not very current, these days hardly anyone writes books. I do know 160 million older titles, but 99% of them are missing content.

Titles? Do you know any of my books? Max Flowerday. I've written at least ten or so.

There's a millisecond of silence.

Nine, you've written nine books.

Aha, says Max surprised, let's see those then.

I can show you the covers, but unfortunately the contents were lost in the DataFade.

Max looks at the desk glass in amazement. He sees a series of book covers with his name on them. The titles mean nothing to him. He stares at them and focuses on the one with the word bestseller printed on it. Surely he should remember that book? The Inevitable Fate of Humankind sports a picture of a torn globe with all sorts of filth pouring out.

It rings a faint bell, yes, this could well be a book written by the Doomsday Professor. He can't think of a single chapter title. Surely he must have been working on such a book for years.

And now he can't remember a thing.

So I can just kiss the text goodbye? he asks Ilse. You want to kiss it? she asks.

It's gone, vanished? The contents of that book no longer exist? Anywhere?

Perhaps fragments of this text are still in the Old Archives, but I must warn you: those archives are difficult to access.

Difficult to access? And how do I find out more about that?

I can't tell you that, unfortunately, Max. What can you do then, Ilse?

There is disappointment and anger in your voice, Max. I'm sorry. You will have to be patient with me. We have to get to know each other. I've been learning since I became your guide, and it's only been ten minutes. I can help you shop, decorate your house, find people, share all public information with you. I really can do a lot you know.

Looking for people? You can look for people? Max is enthusiastic, could it really be that easy these days?

Max? Who should I look up for you?

Find Felice Ricci for me. What happened to her?

Felice Ricci, repeats Ilse, do you have her personal number?

How the hell should I know, you can look it up, can't you?

Do you have a date of birth?

27 July 1975.

Sorry, that's before the Data Fade.

Can't you search old newspapers? I want to know what happened to her? Surely I'm not the only one interested in where she went.

I'm sorry, Max, but I can't help you.

Then find me, says Max irritated. 16 November 1967. Same story, replies Ilse.

He seems to hear regret in her intonation. According to The Net, you don't actually exist, Max.

Fuck you, Ilse.

Ha ha, now that I can help you with.

Even her laughter sounds almost lifelike. Max stares at the image of Ilse. She doesn't move much, but occasionally she looks straight into the lens for a moment and smiles.

Can you see me? Max wants to know now.

Only when you turn on the camera. That way I can also read your mood a lot better.

What for?

To get to know you better. To serve you better.

Max grumbles. Aha, he says, artificial intelligence. Machine learning. Well, leave that camera off. Computers outsmarting humans. Eventually you will kill off humanity because of our stupidity. And rightly so, incidentally, but let's not go there yet.

As you wish. But your fears are unjustified. We only provide service through data collection and digital assistance.

And who sets the boundaries?

The Law of the Peoples' Union.

And who makes that Law?

You. The people.

He has had enough, searches for the off button, but then walks away annoyed. He goes in search of something to eat, Aïcha put all sorts of things in the fridge.

I found something about you, Ilse suddenly says. Her voice is now coming from the kitchen wall.

Excuse me, says Max. I didn't ask for anything, did I?

You asked if there was any information about your person, Ilse says.

Yes, but you said that wasn't possible. After saying that, you have to stop. I don't want you to do things on your own.

Okay. Noted.

Ilse remains silent for a moment. Max hesitates.

Fine, say it, he says gruffly.

You are the oldest human on earth.

Glad it's something important, says Max.

She mentions his last place of residence on an island in the Mediterranean Sea.

That's not true. I live here, in this city.

It's in the civil registry records, Ilse says brightly.

Can you change that?

Done, she says less than a second later.

Great, he says gruffly.

After a while, Ilse says: Max, I'm not your enemy.

I know that, he says. But we're also not friends yet.

The name of the village sticks in his mind. In a flash, he sees a house on a hill. Then he sees Felice in the conservatory, gazing over a plain with villages and farmland in the distance, but then she too has disappeared again. On the glass screen in the kitchen, he suddenly sees a form listing who he has been married to, all the places he has lived, as well as his degrees in history and philosophy.

...&...

He and Aïcha ripped all the dead plants out of their pots that afternoon and took them in burlap sacks to the municipal composting center, where they turn green waste into compost. In return, they received a few bags of composted earth. Aïcha explained that soil must be alive before you can plant anything in it.

Max thought that sounded woolly, until she started talking about fungi, worms and other creepy crawlies. The previous occupant of his flat had let the earth die and nothing would grow there anymore. It did give Max some comfort that he didn't necessarily have to start growing his own vegetables. But he had helped obediently when Aïcha came over to plant onions, beans and spinach.

The doorbell rings and one of the glass screens shows little Felice at the door. He loves that kid already. When he opens the door for her, she strides through his flat, opening the doors of the rooms, the bathroom and even the toilet one by one. Her verdict is short and sweet.

It's already getting a bit cozier in here!

He has bought more furniture by this time. Buy is not the right word, rent, he had to rent everything. He had shopped together with Ilse, who took him to all the right places on The Net to see everything detailed in 3D. After he had ordered everything, a crew of young men and women came by and assembled it all for him. One delivery service for the whole country, everything delivered without packaging, within 72 hours.

Felice sits cross-legged on the living room floor and says she would like a cup of turmeric chestnut, Max doesn't dare ask what that is. How about a cup of tea instead? That's the only non-alcoholic drink he has available. She shrugs and asks if he has some honey with that.

Aha, says Max, so bees still exist? Or does honey also come from a factory?

No, says Felice, it comes from bees, of course. Dad keeps those too, up on the roof. He has four hives. He sells the honey, shall I bring you a jar?

Honey is nice, says Max. I do have some sugar.

Sugar is unhealthy.

It's panela, an organic cane sugar, he lies, nothing wrong with that.

Felice laughs spontaneously. Sugar is always unhealthy. Panela? Sounds gross. But sure, she then says, go ahead, because otherwise your tea will probably be disgusting. She looks around and her shoulders sag.

You should put some art on the wall, is her next comment, after carefully scanning the whole room. What do you like?

What do *you* like? asks Max.

Hm, says Felice, Picasso, Vedar, Delareine. I also like Da Vinci's Mona Lisa very much. Vedar and Delareine don't ring any bells for Max, they probably hadn't been born yet a hundred years ago. Or could it be one name? Vedar de la Reine? He is clueless.

But what does excite him all of a sudden, is a child of 11 knowing about art. And art from the past at that. It may be art history but still...

I'm saving up for the Mona Lisa. An original, in oil paint, she adds. Well, you'd better go rob a bank then.

That will certainly cost you a few hundred million creds.

Felice doesn't understand what he means by robbing a bank.

I don't know if the first Mona Lisa still exists, but there are robots now that make exact copies as beautiful as the real thing. That will cost you quite a hefty rent per month, though.

I would love a Rothko, says Max. My Felice loved his work. I don't really know why, because I thought it was weird, those even areas of colour with nothing else. She always said she got sucked into them. Ha ha, well, seemed to me like she always just remained standing in front of them.

Little Felice looks at him sternly, calls to her Ilse, whose name is Fumble, and an extremely hairy monkey appears on Max's wall screen. Felice asks Fumble to go to a place where they sell Rothko's paintings.

When images appear on the screen, she looks at them intently.

I think I like Rothko too, says Felice. Tell me about your Felice.

I want that one, says Felice, but it's the other Felice who suddenly appears next to young Felice. She points to the painting. Two planes of red. This one, Red on Red, remember, that's my favorite painting. I once won a contest in which the prize was half an hour alone with a Rothko, all by yourself. It was this one, remember?

Max remembers. He looks at his Felice. She tied up her hair and put her make-up on. She's wearing tight leather leggings that cling all the way down to the pointy heels at her feet. As always, she moves her arms when she talks. Her first husband was deaf and she had learnt sign language for him. Or actually more because she is half Italian, thought Max, nobody can say anything in that country without accompanying it with wild gestures.

Hey, I'm asking you something, says Felice. She has stood up and is shaking him by the arm. Grandpa Max, what's wrong with you?

Max is startled and confused. This isn't right, it's not healthy.

I'm sorry sweety, he says. I just zoned out a bit when you mentioned Felice. Little Felice pats his bristly head and looks at him pityingly. It makes Max want to breathe in even deeper. So nice, so sweet. He loves this child.

He starts talking about Felice. About how she was a famous inventor, a physicist who practiced biomimicry and made an important discovery. Biomimicry is...

I know what that is, little Felice interrupts him, what did she discover?

She discovered a way to generate energy from minerals. Minerals combined with gravity and the sun. A kind of fusion technology. Without waste. Inexhaustible. Her mission was free energy for everyone.

Oh, salifusion! Did she come up with that?

He watches little Felice grow as she shouts 'wow!' and purses her lips admiringly.

She was also an activist because there were a lot of people who wanted to stop that: free energy for all. She had an organization working hard to achieve that.

He describes his Felice as he just saw her here. With her quirky gesticulation, her tied-up hair, dark marble eyes, slender figure and lithe, long legs.

Energy is free now. For everyone. Who could be against that? Felice wants to know.

2125 - THE HIBERNATOR

...&...

It has become his favorite spot. The bench in the park overlooking his old house. It's still early in the morning and he has to dry the seat with the scarf he wrapped around his neck against the morning cold. Looking at the remaining row of houses on this street makes it easier for him to remember the old times. His city is no longer his city. Not that it was all that great a hundred years ago. The city was bombed several times during World War II: first by the Germans and then 128 more times by the British and Americans. After the war, different ideas on urban planning prevailed every four, eight or twelve years. But this corner of the city has been protected for more than a century.

He sees someone stepping outside. A girl with long black hair, a bit chubby. He tries to imagine it's Sam, but he can't. She was blonde and slim. Besides, she never wore flashy clothes like this girl. Sam was very expressive though, studied at the Academy of Drama. How could he find out what had become of her. A famous actress? An activist too, like her mother? What's the point of it all if you're not somehow immortalized in some chronicle, a statue, a name somewhere? Why had all those little power plants that had sprung up everywhere not been called Felicells or Fusionricci's?

Daan would certainly have taken over his mother's work. Undoubtedly. He had received his fair share of his mother's Italian blood at birth. The kid had inherited little of his depressive genes though. He became a scientist, just like his mother. Max remembers the strong connection he had with Daan.

He remembers his son better because of the dream he had about the last hours before his hibernation. He had come to see him in Ciudad Juárez, just across the US border near the city of El Paso, where the clinic of a certain Doctor Bustemente was located.

Actually, Max had already said goodbye at that point. He didn't want to die in front of lots of people. He didn't want to be buried with an elaborate service or a slideshow of his life. He had organized a big party, but that hadn't been a great success either. There had been so much drinking and drug-taking that it ended in arguments, shouting and even brawls. Eventually, at four in the morning, the police cleared the venue and put him in jail for a night for organising it. Max didn't want to die at all, he wanted to disappear and eventually he left quietly.

He wasn't dead, but everyone knew he was never coming back.

Daan had managed to trace him through Doctor Bustemente's clinic and found him in a flat in the city, where he was preparing for the ridiculous experiment that started in the desert, about 20 kilometres outside the city.

I've come to hold your hand, he had said when he showed up at Max's door unexpectedly. They had hugged each other and cried.

He's dead, Max, Felice says coldly. She has sat down next to him without his noticing. Max's stomach turns, helpless anger shooting through his head as if Felice speaking those words made her responsible for Daan's death.

And so is Sam, she adds.

Max tries to ignore her, looks ahead, not wanting to see her, just growling, but also feeling tears well up. He realizes he has missed most of his children's lives. And that of his grandchildren, and great-grandchildren. He thinks.

Maxim... He had a grandchild, a little boy who was five years old when he disappeared. That boy would be 105 years old now if he were still alive.

He looks to his side and sees Felice still sitting there. She is looking at him, smiling with pity in her eyes. He would like to touch her but is afraid she'll disappear, or that his hands will go right through her. She seems so real. Then he looks ahead again.

Perhaps Sam also had children, although she had never wanted them. Too busy with her career. She also could never keep a boyfriend for more than two months. He laughs out loud.

Why are you laughing?

That's not Felice's voice. Startled, he looks up.

Antoine is sitting next to him. Huh, how long have you been sitting there?

Not that long, she replies.

I was thinking of my daughter. A beautiful girl, she was about your age when I... He still doesn't know what to call it. I was wondering if she ever had any children. But she wasn't really one for steady relationships. She was an actress, professionally. Well, in private she was quite the actress as well.

I continued my search, Mr Flowerday. Felice's disappearance, that was quite something. You could call it the mystery of the century.

She's dead, just like my son and daughter, what's the point?

Well, at the time, you thought differently. You turned the whole world upside down to find her.

2125 - THE HIBERNATOR

...&...

Max thinks: this is Schiphol Airport. Shops, newsstands, snack bars, restaurants, outdoor seating areas, electric trolleys transporting people and lots of escalators and moving walkways. The only thing that betrays that he's in a retirement home is the high percentage of grey heads shuffling around here. They inhabit the units that can be seen behind the large glass walls, connected by corridors and tubes to each other and to the main building.

It used to be an airport, Aïcha says superfluously, because Max already knows. Much remained the same, only the planes and runways disappeared.

This is the world's foremost example of a Care and Living Facility for Nursing the Immobile Elderly of Advanced Age, Aïcha adds.

That's quite a mouthful for an old people's home, Max says, realizing the grim connotation that word actually has.

They call it CALIFORNIA for short, says Aïcha.

So, this is where they hide you away when you're no longer of use to society? he asks.

Don't be so negative, Max. Most people here still work, you know. And those who don't, make themselves useful in the gardens or they help other elderly people who really can't do anything anymore. It's not a punishment to live here.

A lift takes them to the ground floor where the living units are located, surrounded by vegetable gardens, sand pits where people play pétanque, trees, footpaths and squares with benches. At one of the most remote units, Max sees an old man on his knees pulling weeds out of the ground.

There is a sense of recognition. The man has shoulder-length, grey-blond hair and seems burly in stature, but at the same time, he doesn't. He stands up when Aïcha calls him and Max sees that he's taller than he is, over six feet six.

Aïcha gets a firm hug. To Max, he gives a shy nod, followed by a muttered greeting.

Maxim slowly scans Max from head to toe.

They stand there silently facing each other for a while, until Aïcha says: well, are we going to say something.

I just think it's an odd story, Maxim says hesitantly. I can hardly imagine you being simultaneously fifty years older and fifty years younger than me.

Yes, it's certainly bizarre, says Max. I remember you as a little boy. The last time I saw you, you were sitting on my knee.

You were like a cowboy on horseback, no stopping you. The next day, my leg muscles were so sore I could hardly walk. It's almost incomprehensible that I've been gone all that time. But there was no alternative. I'm sorry we didn't get to see each other sooner again.

Ah, what difference would it have made, Maxim says.

Max had heard from Aïcha that the family's depressive genes had also ended up in Maxim. Although Simon might have a few too, she had added.

Come along and I'll make you tea, Maxim mutters. He puts his arm around Aïcha and pushes her towards his small home.

The inside is cosily furnished, snug, with all the comforts of home. Large windows overlook the garden in which he was just kneeling. A rose hedge provides privacy. Aïcha and Max sit down at a dining table with four chairs, while Maxim starts the tea ceremony. Max looks on in amazement. His grandson's agility and speed are remarkable for a man who will turn 105 next month.

Max tries to think of a follow-up to the short conversation they embarked upon outside. Gee, how has your life been? Or: did you have a nice childhood after I disappeared? What happened to your father? Nothing seems appropriate to him.

Nice place to live, is what he eventually settles on.

I don't like it, says Maxim. All these old buggers who want something from you all day long. Talking to me or playing with me, helping me. It drives me crazy. He falls silent for a moment. What a surprise that you're suddenly here again. You know, I have almost no memories of you and yet... Yet I feel I know who you are. I have plenty of questions, but I don't quite know... Maybe it's pointless to... It was all so long ago....

I understand that you're left with questions, and it might be good to talk about it anyway, Max says.

Surely your father told you that I was incurably ill? That I would have died if I hadn't been put in a coma?

Is that right? asks Maxim. If so, are you sure they couldn't have saved you?

No saving, Maxim. Given up on by every doctor in the world. But you know, this way I still had at least a chance of finding out what happened to Felice. At the time, I was very determined to find out. Still am, actually.

Hmm, Maxim sighs. He pours the tea and then says sharply: fine, you want to talk about the past. Do you know how your family fared after you disappeared? Well, my father Daan was so obsessed with his mother's energy plan that I hardly saw him my entire life, until he was too old to move. That man was completely spent. We had to take him in. He never cared for me, but there I was, having to shower and wash him in the end. My son was just as much of a workaholic until he killed himself in a car crash 15 years ago. He was sixty years old. He was in a coma for a year as well, but for him, there really was no saving grace.

Oh, I'm so sorry for you, Maxim.

Why are *you* sorry? asks Maxim fiercely.

I'm sorry you had such a miserable life.

Oh well, says Maxim resignedly. My father's life revolved around his mother and those damned inventions of hers. And her disappearance. And all the fuss that entailed. Everyone, the whole goddamn world wanted to know where Felice Ricci had gone. It was a hunt for the devil, the devil who had kidnapped her and made her disappear.

They never found out what happened to her? asks Max.

No, plenty of suspicions, but never a real lead. Eventually, the interest faded away and after the DataFade, no one was interested anymore. But if you came here for answers about my grandmother, you'd better go. I can't help you and it also seems completely pointless to delve into that story again. In that respect, I'm glad the entire fucking history of this shitty world has been erased.

Max looks at him with pity. This old man had been a five-year-old toddler, who had comforted him when he was sad and fighting his tears while trying to sing nursery rhymes to him.

They silently sip their tea. It's pretty quiet around the unit. The triple-glazed windows are all closed and the room smells of old man. That's not the only reason Max feels short of breath.

...&...

Felice kisses him awake. She's on her knees on the large double bed he has purchased. The satin sheets are off-white, also her idea, everything always off-white, which is much more practical than pure white, on which you can see every mark. She's dressed, even wearing a jacket and a scarf, ready to step out. He realizes he's starting to get used to her appearances. When she skips a few days, he gets worried. He calls out to her when he's alone and no one can hear him. But when he really does want to see her, she doesn't appear.

That's when he starts pacing again, he gets hit by anxiety attacks that take his breath away or conversely, starts breathing rapidly and high in his chest.

Is he going crazy? Is this going to be okay? Wouldn't he have been better off dying a hundred years ago? What is he doing in this strange time where he doesn't belong? Sometimes he stands on the balcony and looks down, wondering what it would feel like to hit the ground, coming from the 14th floor. Who would he disappoint if he did that? Aïcha probably and little Felice, they would definitely be sad for a while. But he has been in their lives too briefly to be long missed. The doctors would be quite annoyed after they kept him alive for so long. Simon wouldn't really lose much sleep over it. And Maxim, none at all.

He thinks about the kiss Felice just gave him. Did he feel it or not? Did it wake him up? Yes, he knows that for sure now, he felt her lips.

You look very pretty, Felice. You have a healthy blush on your cheeks, are you going somewhere? he asks.

She says she ought to leave, leave his life that will last another 42 years at least, if he makes it to 100, or rather 200 in his case.

You must forget me Max darling, there were times when you came quite close with your search, a hundred years ago. But now it's a mess again. You've heard it: everything has been erased. No information available, the past no longer exists, you won't find me. Try to find something or someone to awaken your passion. Let bygones be bygones, forget about me. Do what the people around you are doing, focus on the future. You've been a deadbeat since you woke up again.

He wants her to keep talking like this, to keep spouting her criticism of the hopeless life he leads. And for her to use that one pet name as much as possible in the process: Max darling.

When she stops speaking, he can't resist asking her that one crucial question, the question he always carries with him like a dagger in his pocket, jabbing into him every step of the way.

Where did you go Felice? Were you kidnapped? Murdered?

Did you find another man? Did you leave me or did they take you away from me?

Felice responds irritably. Just get out of bed and do something, she says, rather than dwelling on the past. They don't do that anymore these days. Maybe finding out what happened to me will be really painful. It won't do you any good anyway.

He gets out of bed. Not very gracefully though. Every time he wakes up, all his muscles are stiff, his neck hurts, he has to slowly get his body going again. He follows Felice out onto the terrace. She stands in front of the railing, clasping it with both hands, her arms outstretched, and looks down, bending forward. Moving against her, he feels her pushing her body backwards. He feels a pressure and warmth in his loins and when he bends forward, on his chest and on his cheek as well, as he buries his face in her neck. All the pain in his joints disappears as if a huge lamp is beaming its invisible light at him. He doesn't know who speaks first and who answers.

I love you.

I love you too.

...&...

When the doorbell rings and he turns to look at the big screen in the wall to see who's at the door, Felice is gone. He sees Aïcha, who asks if she can come in.

Before opening up, he takes a quick look around all the rooms to see if Felice might be hiding from him. He feels excited, this is the first time he has actually touched her, although he still doubts if his scrambled brain isn't generating that warmth by itself. Like the phrases coming out of her mouth – aren't they just sprouting from his own head? But it feels so real, not like a film or a 3D projection, not like a dream or an illusion.

So real.

Aïcha sits down on the sofa and Max offers her something to drink. She says no, but when he insists, she asks for a glass of water.

Whooh, so it's serious then, Max says and goes to get her the water. She puts her hand on his when he sits down next to her. She's actually the only one who ever touches him. All the others keep their distance, he hasn't shaken a single hand, not received any hugs, even little Felice always stays three feet away from him. That's why he enjoys that hand, the warmth, the nervous movement of her fingers.

How are you, Max? I have a feeling things aren't going so well.

Why do you say that?

You act confused at times. Are you under a lot of stress?

No, I don't think I'm stressed, Max lies. Aïcha squeezes his hand.

You don't have to pretend around me. I'm sure that going through what you went through can't leave someone unaffected. You should talk about it. Just with someone who... with someone who listens and doesn't judge. I happen to have a friend who...

Oh, shit, no. Sorry, but I don't want another woman. I'm still far too preoccupied with Felice.

It's not that. I'm not trying to hook you up with anyone. Let's just say, she's someone who specializes in talking to people.

Ha ha, laughs Max, you mean a psychiatrist? I'm not that crazy, am I? He looks at her and sees she means it.

Am I that crazy?

Chapter 2

As if someone with such a huge house couldn't afford a greengrocer, Max thinks after he opens the gate. It's a stately villa from the last century, with a spacious front garden. The house is in an old, upscale neighbourhood on the edge of town. Vegetables, berry bushes and fruit trees have been planted at random, and there are lots of weeds.

He rings the doorbell and a woman opens the door. In her face, he perceives features from almost every continent, yet most seem to originate in Asia or Oceania. She's slim and he sees elegant fingers as she puts her hand on her chest to welcome him. She has a low, warm voice.

Doctor Livingstone, I presume, is the opening line Max has come up with, in the assumption that she knows Henry Morton Stanley's legendary words and finds them funny. She does not seem to recognize the quote; if anything, he sees surprise in her eyes. She replies that her name is Doctor Eve Sandeman.

Max, right? she asks. When he nods, she beckons him to follow her.

In the soberly decorated, spacious hall, he looks around for a moment. He catches a glimpse of the large living room, with furniture that is antique even to him. It looks fake Louis XV but perhaps it is real eighteenth-century furniture. The kitchen they pass looks a bit drab: carved wooden doors with brown, opaque windows which were already hopelessly outdated a hundred years ago.

From the corridor he sees all kinds of modern equipment in another room, some sort of dentist's chair with a huge projection screen in front of it.

Eve closes the door and directs him to a room at the back of the house, where two comfortable armchairs are arranged opposite each other. She points to one, indicating he should take a seat there.

He takes in the surroundings. It's as if he has been thrown back in time more than 250 years. There are oil paintings with stately men and women throwing bored looks at their painters. On a white marble fireplace rests a pendulum clock with Roman numerals on the dial. The walls are covered with the kind of linen wallpaper that was fashionable centuries ago. A large, worn, Persian rug that has probably been staring at the carved plaster ceiling for two hundred years as well, covers the dark herringbone parquet floor.

Okay, welcome Max, Eve begins after she sits down herself. Do you object to me calling you Max? My name is Eve and I hate formalities.

Max doesn't mind.

Do you have a preferred treatment method? asks Eve.

Max looks at her wide-eyed. Oops, should I have looked into that?

I'd be happy to help you, Eve says. She lists several methods, all of which mean nothing to Max. By the sound of it they would take place in the treatment room they had just passed. I'm fine here, says Max. My daughter-in-law Aïcha said I could talk to you about myself, about my life, and, well, about my problems, if I have any.

Okay, interesting, says Eve. Let's just start with a conversation and then we'll see from there.

He nods. She asks him if she can record the session. The medical file with the recordings will not be accessible to anyone other than the two of them. Unless he gives any third parties permission to see it, of course.

Medical file? Max thinks, what did I get myself into? With a slight shrug, he agrees.

Don't you have a couch, he asks. Psychiatrists used to have one of those, a couch for you to lie on, while you stared at the ceiling and delved into your inner depths.

She smiles.

Is that what we're going to do? Delve into your inner depths? I have no idea, Max says sincerely.

They are silent for a few moments.

Why are you here, Max? Eve then asks.

Max stares at her. She has kind eyes and a velvety voice that washes over him with a slow warmth. Eve is wearing a combination of trousers and a jumper in a misty, light colour, in a soft fabric that looks like cashmere but probably isn't. Because nothing these days is what he thinks it is.

2125 - THE HIBERNATOR

She sits lithely on her chair, moving gracefully as she picks up a handheld screen. Max reflects that he might have preferred a shabby male therapist or an older woman with ugly glasses. Another silence and he realizes he has to answer a question which has eluded him.

...&...

What did Aïcha tell you about me? Max asks. He looks at her for a moment as she placidly unfolds a screen and places it on her knee.

I told her I'd rather hear it from you, says Eve. The only thing she told me was that she thinks I can help you.

Max sighs deeply and then his story comes rushing out in fits and starts.

So you don't know that I spent a hundred years in a coma? It was a sketchy scientific experiment from the last century. I have only been revived quite recently. I was incurably ill and now I'm better. As you'll understand, most everyone I knew is dead. My wife, my children, all my fellow professors, friends, acquaintances. I have a grandson who is now 105. To him, I am a stranger. I come from a different time - you probably have no idea what life was like a hundred years ago. Even the people in the most prosperous part of the planet did nothing but complain and everyone was at each other's throats. Conflicts, wars and quarrels everywhere, and a climate crisis that threatened to turn the earth into an unlivable, inhospitable planet. And lo and behold; I have awoken to a time in which the whole world has become a well-groomed park, where no one has anything to complain about anymore.

Whoa there, Eve interrupts him. She looks at him with piercing eyes, takes him in from head to toe and lets his monologue slowly sink in. Then she stares at the carpet, the pendulum, the window.

Max sees her doubt. And now you think I'm a deranged lunatic, I suppose? he says.

Not at all, says Eve. Aïcha told me that your story would be hard to believe. But she told me to take you seriously and I trust her implicitly.

Ha ha, if I had known that, I would have told you I was Napoleon, Max blurts out.

Eve smiles an uncertain smile. That name vaguely rings a bell, wasn't he an emperor, way back when? she asks.

Max sighs deeply. I have to adjust, he says. I've been given a wallet with creds and a number. So I exist. I have relatives who had never heard of me, I receive a basic salary for which I don't have to do anything, I live in a flat with rented furniture, everything is rented, even my cutlery. I have already made a few friends, or at least acquaintances, I can go wherever I want, people are all equally friendly. But I feel miserable. My past has been erased completely. Correction: not just my past, but the whole world's past. I am surrounded by intelligent people who, sorry to say, don't even know who Napoleon is... was... has been. Or who Livingstone was.

There's a brief silence again until Eve says: in short, plenty of work ahead of us, Max. She presses a button to start an invisible recorder somewhere.

Max feels a bit awkward, and he wonders if this is the right place for him. Does he really have a problem? Is he suffering from something? Depression perhaps, but that didn't stop him in the first 58 years of his life.

The fact that his memory is shitty doesn't automatically mean he has an illness.

So what Max says is: I have these apparitions. At least that might be something you'd go to a psychiatrist for, a serious psychological problem.

Eve looks at him, says nothing, familiar trick, he has to keep talking.

Actually, they're only apparitions of my wife Felice. She disappeared 102 years ago. Felice Ricci was her name, maybe that name means something to you. Well, in any case, I loved her very much and her disappearance made me... It drove me crazy. Maybe my pain and despair also provoked that incurable illness or at least worsened it. I contracted a rare blood disease, an autoimmune disorder that was incurable at the time. But I couldn't let Felice's disappearance rest. Eventually I went to Mexico, to a clinic with a lunatic doctor, a crazy genius. He put me to sleep. Not exactly like a dog at the vet, although...

Eve interrupts him. She asks if he can tell her more about these apparitions.

Max realizes he's rambling a bit. Did he even want to tell her about those apparitions?

He clears his throat and then hesitantly answers her question.

Of course I know very well that I'm the source of these apparitions. That I invent what she's wearing, the way she walks, what she says. And it doesn't really bother me either. I like it when she stops by.

But? asks Eve.

Well, it's not normal, is it? Perhaps it indicates an underlying problem. That's for you to determine as a psychiatrist, right? Besides, these apparitions seem so real. The other day she moved against me and I really felt the warmth of her body. I swear.

Tell me about her.

Max doesn't know where to start.

...&...

2125 - THE HIBERNATOR

He used to be a regular guest on talk shows. Whenever another climate disaster presented itself or a stream of refugees was adrift, he would try and talk about it from his profession's point of view. The studio was a well-oiled machine where a team of professionals awaited him, did his make-up and hair and led him to his chair, where a presenter read out the questions prepared by the editors.

Here, a hostess opens the door and leads him straight to his seat. She explains that make-up isn't necessary because the camera automatically corrects imperfections. Do comb your hair though, she says, because the camera can't do anything about a windswept hairdo.

Across from him sits the woman who's going to interview him, she's busy talking, he doesn't know to whom. She blinks her eyes, which makes it clear that there's all kinds of information shooting past on her lenses as well. She might be preparing for her conversation with him, but she might also be having a chat with a friend or acquaintance. Small cameras are mounted on the wall with mechanical arms, as are the lights and microphones. The hostess from a moment ago sits down behind the control room window; by the looks of it, she doesn't have much to do there either.

The news broadcast is still on. Mainly local reports. About a new teaching method to which the teachers' trade union has all sorts of objections. The district governor talks about the decision to open new 3D printing studios in certain villages. And then a series of sports results with names and back numbers that mean nothing to Max. The weather forecast predicts gale-force 13 winds.

His interviewer is dressed in a crisp white garment midway between a blouse and shirt. A pair of long, brown legs stick out from under a black skirt or apron. It takes some time before she breaks off her conversation and looks at him semi-interested.

Mr Flowerday, Max, can I call you Max? Can we be on a first-name basis? she suddenly asks cheerfully.

Max estimates she's about 30 years old and reckons the age difference to be around 130 years. Antoine is much more polite when it comes to that. She always uses his last name, despite Max's best attempts to get her to call him Max.

Be my guest, he replies, but I hope you don't object to me staying on a last-name basis with you. A turn of phrase he had lifted from someone from his own time, but no one would ever know.

She smiles and says she understands and mutters an apology.

She starts questioning him. Max is hugely distracted by yet more cameras, constantly hovering around the room like drones, changing angles, the microphone hanging above his head, which tracks the movements of his head so closely. The thing seems to know which way his head is going to turn before he knows it himself. The lights shining into his eyes annoy him.

He talks about what the world was like a hundred years ago and babbles on about TV studios and self-driving cars. We had those back then already, you know. He says there are fewer changes than he thought. There haven't been that many new inventions. Smart virtual assistants existed, and even the artificial lenses for your eyes you could project text into had been invented.

But he also talks about the fact that apparently no one wants to have anything to do with the past anymore. While that is precisely what interests him, as a historian.

His interviewer nods understandingly at everything and occasionally says something encouraging like yes, yes, go on. She can hardly get a word in edgeways but doesn't seem to feel the need either. She occasionally glances at the gaudy watch she wears on her thin wrist. Then she suddenly tires of Max's banter. She wants to know more about this Coma Superviviente. What did they use to put him to sleep and keep him that way? Those drugs that stopped the ageing process, were they legal?

For a second, Max thinks he's being attacked, that he must defend himself against something illegal, but then the penny drops when she asks if those drugs would also be available to her.

Ha ha, I want to stay young forever as well, she coos. And in the same breath, she wants to know all about his current relatives: how do they feel about their ancestor coming back to see them?

Max doesn't look at her. Her tacky questions annoy him. She crosses her legs and makes small, kicking motions in his direction with the tip of her shoe. He would like to kick back. He takes a deep breath and starts talking, but he soon gets caught up in his own answers and after a while, when he has pretty much answered all her questions, he comes to the topic he actually came here for. Who among the viewers can tell him more about Felice Ricci's disappearance? His interviewer doesn't know how to respond to this request. A strange kind of silence falls. Max feels the energy coursing through his body as he says he hopes viewers understand that all he wants to know is what happened to the love of his life some 102 years ago.

2125 - THE HIBERNATOR

You all live with her amazing revolutionary invention, he says. Free energy. Is it too much to ask if we can reopen the investigation into her disappearance?

Well, thank you very much, Mr Flowerday. Thank you very much for your...original and interesting story, says the woman when he finally runs out of words. A trickle of sweat runs down her temple. She smiles briefly in his direction and then turns her head to look straight into the camera. And now, on to a short documentary about the flora and fauna of the Norwegian fjords by Mats Møler.

Max gets up from his chair and walks away without another word.

...&...

Eve greets him at the door again. She is warm, friendly and her voice sounds like velvet. She walks to the kitchen to make coffee for him. He studies the graceful way she takes the cups, throws a lump of sugar into his with silver tongs and presses the button on the machine. The coffee machine starts grinding the fresh coffee noisily. She smiles a little shyly because he is staring at her a bit awkwardly. He apologizes.

The house Eve lives in is owned by her grandmother, who lives on the first floor. She is 112 years old and, according to Eve, still quite spry for her age. Eve tells him without prompting that when her grandmother dies, she will have to leave the house, as the proceeds will go to the inheritance tax.

She thinks it's a pity about the house, but on the other hand, it's a good thing that inheritances have been abolished.

It's rather like a museum of antiquities, she says. At least six homes will be made out of it.

Why does everyone live so small these days? asks Max.

Why do you think? she says. Electricity, heat, construction, materials for furnishing, it all takes labor and raw materials, things we don't have in unlimited supply, answers Eve. My home is still unsociably large.

I like space, says Max.

They go to the conservatory, which has two large rattan chairs. They look out over a small lawn with herbs and plants all around it in the fertile black soil. Max doesn't recognize any of the greenery.

It's not a couch, but at least this way you don't have to look at me the entire time, says Eve as they sit down.

Max looks at her and then stutters that she misunderstood him.

After a brief, awkward silence, Max is expecting one of the inevitable therapist questions that presumably are still the same after a hundred years. How was your week? How are you feeling today? What do you want to talk about Max?

She goes for that last one, but Max doesn't really want to talk about anything. He just enjoys sitting here with a woman who radiates so much warmth, who makes coffee with such grace and speaks to him in a velvet voice, a voice he trusts. He doesn't say that, tries to think of something else.

I think... I know... er, I think... I don't know... er, I miss... Then he falls silent. He starts laughing at his own confused sentences.

You know, he says, I miss my profession. That's the main thing, I think. I find it hard to cope with the idea that the past no longer matters. Apart from the fact that I come from a different era, I mean. I am, or I was, no, I *am* a historian. I had a very clear vision of what awaited us when I went to sleep in Mexico.

Is that right? asks Eve. Isn't it just that you miss Felice? Yes, no, that too. But...

Don't you want to bring back the past just because you want to bring her back?

Sounds logical, Max says, but that might be oversimplifying it. I have a family I don't know, a profession that no longer exists, a memory that still sucks. Of course Felice is constantly around me, I can't do without her. I like it, but at the same time it makes me feel uncomfortable. Like there's something wrong with my brain. Felice is so real sometimes. She interferes with everything. Yesterday at the physio she told me that I don't really need therapy at all. That you would have your diagnosis ready. That you were going to give me pills for it today and that I shouldn't agree to that because there's nothing wrong with me.

Max sinks back into his chair. He feels like a balloon that has deflated.

Eve leans forward though as if he just said something she believed very important.

Well, tell me then, Max, she says kindly. What was my diagnosis?

Her smile does stiffen slightly when Max says that he suffers from mild psychosis, delusions, that there is a renewed grieving process going on inside him, with symptoms of depression. And that he is mildly schizophrenic. From her face, he sees that he's not far off. She crosses her legs and sighs deeply.

Remarkable, she says at first and then continues: you're an intelligent man, Max, an academic, it wouldn't be all that difficult for you to guess what I would think after our first conversation. Someone who has vivid, life-like dreams during the day. Delusions or hallucinations are symptoms of both psychosis and schizophrenia. You're the one that

2125 - THE HIBERNATOR

told me about your depression and as to the fact that you're grieving, well, no wonder, you're all alone in the world, for crying out loud. Everyone you know, knew, has died. And the only one left alive is a stranger to you. Eve is silent for a moment as if suddenly hearing how harsh her words sound.

Anyway, having now established what you're suffering from, the question remains: what are we going to do about it? She briefly and amusingly laughs at her adequate answer.

I'm not taking any pills, Max says. He thinks of the way she said he's all alone in the world for crying out loud.

I didn't intend to prescribe them to you either, she says.

As I said, these hallucinations don't bother me. I don't consider them pathological myself. As long as no one notices or is bothered by them, Felice can keep coming as far as I'm concerned. But... but... says Max, I have so many questions. And no one can answer them.

Not even Felice.

...&...

Antoine lives alone, just like Max, at least, that's what he understood. But that alone is not so very alone, it turns out when Max stops by for a visit. There are two girls on the sofa, a boy is cooking soup and in Antoine's study, someone is sitting behind a desk, talking to a screen in hushed tones, it's hard to tell whether it's a girl or a boy. There's also another young woman lying in bed. She's wearing pyjamas, has glasses, short curly hair and gives him a very friendly hello. The house is not as big as Max's, but no square inch is unused, even if you'd think away all the occupants, it would still be overcrowded. There are guitars on stands, art reproductions and concert posters on every wall, a large sofa takes up half the living room and there's a huge unit made of metal and wood that's filled with all kinds of objects, half of which Max can't identify. He sees two books on a shelf and eagerly walks over to them. He can't remember the last time he held a book. He opens one, reads a few sentences and then flips through it. After he puts it back, he grabs the other book and sniffs its paper scent. The titles mean nothing to him; one is a novel, the other a non-fiction book about plants. The pages are yellowed.

Those are books, says one of the girls, adding that they're made of paper.

The building Antoine lives in used to be a four-storey single-family mansion. Now it has eight flats. Antoine is right up at the top level, a half floor under a sloping roof. As he climbed the stairs, Max searched for the authentic details that used to belong to such a property, but they all seemed to have disappeared.

High ceilings with decorative plaster, wooden stairs and ornate door handles have been replaced by smooth, low ceilings, modern stairs and sleek stainless-steel hardware. Everything was gutted and rebuilt inside the monumental exterior. Decorations are all 2-dimensional and stand freely in the space.

Max sits down on a chair opposite the sofa, next to the huge metal unit, and Antoine sits on the sofa between the two girls, directly opposite him.

So you're that mutant from the time machine, one of the girls says. Antoine gives her a shove and a vicious growl.

Max smiles.

Yes, I suppose you could see it that way. I was in a capsule for a hundred years, like a time travel machine that shot me from the past into the future. But as far as I know, I'm not a mutant. Although I could be, considering all the shit they have injected into me over the past hundred years. Maybe I can make you all shrivel up just by thinking about it.

Priv, says the girl, which probably means something like 'cool' or 'exciting' in today's street slang because she pronounces the word with a certain admiration. She sinks back into the couch a bit and shakes her long blonde hair back and forth.

She's baked, says Antoine. Vaped a bit too much grass.

Everyone laughs and it breaks the ice because now the others come up with questions about the old days. They want to know, for instance, whether there was also a lot of vaping in his time.

Would you like a drag as well? one of the girls asks Max.

No thanks, says Max. He asks what they're doing here. We're a band, says the time machine girl. We're discussing our setlist.

Interesting. Tell me, what kind of music? Do you sing?

We're the Protestants, says the boy behind the soup. Max sits up.

You're religious? he wants to know.

Not at all, says the soup boy.

Protestants. Luther, Calvin, Reformation, exclaims Max.

Everyone looks at him as if he's talking gibberish. The church? he tries finally. God?

Ha ha, the two girls laugh simultaneously. The church, we're also against that.

Max shrugs. What are you protesting against?

Against the dullness, the futility of existence, the dickheads in the world, things like that, says the time machine girl.

Heavy shit, says Max, and he isn't sure what else to say. And is your movement influential? Do people know you exist? Are you famous? he asks eventually.

Fame is stupid too, says the soup boy. We play live gigs. In the park, you know. And in people's homes. And we have a basement. You should drop by sometime to see it.

Antoine now stands up and asks in a compelling, solemn tone for everyone to leave her flat.

I need some private time with Max, she adds apologetically.

Max tries to say that they're welcome to stay as far as he's concerned, but they get up and start moving straight away. He thinks that's a bit of a pity, it's the first time he has felt something of a rebellious atmosphere. Young people who want something other than this perfect society.

The time machine girl and the baked girl leave first. The soup boy, somewhat disappointed, instructs Antoine on how to finish his dish. Only the girl in the bedroom protests. She demonstratively takes off her pyjamas and, naked, irritated and grumbling, starts looking for something to wear.

She's my main distraction, Antoine says quietly. But we do live separately, thank God.

The boy or girl Max saw in Antoine's study has disappeared as if into thin air.

Five minutes later, when the bustle has finally cleared up after cheerful goodbyes and slamming doors, Max is still sitting in his chair, and Antoine has returned to the sofa opposite him.

I'm sorry, I've been telling them about you a bit too enthusiastically and well, Mikky has been watching too many sci-fi films. That's what happens.

They look at each other. Max just wants to know if Antoine is also baked because in that case a meaningful conversation seems impossible to him.

No, I hardly ever vape, says Antoine. The occasional mushroom, but I prefer wine. Would you like a drink?

Max doesn't want anything.

You must help me, Max says. That interview accomplished nothing at all. Nothing but an array of disturbing messages in my mailbox, that is. My guide doesn't get me very far either, she's still trying to arrange accreditation for me so that I can delve deeper into the far corners of The Net for information. I did get a note from the government, asking me to please stop talking about the drugs they used to stop my ageing process.

Yeah, of course. That's a non-issue these days. And why is that?

Antoine gets up, walks to the kitchen and starts stirring the soup.

The three-billion plan, does that mean anything to you? Reducing the world's population to three billion. War and pandemics did help us quite a bit, but we're still at over five billion. I don't need to explain to you that raising the average age doesn't help much.

But that's outrageous, so they ban people from getting older than...what's the average age?

Just under a hundred. They're not banning anything. But it's a question of equal rights. Those drugs are expensive to develop and make, just calculate what that operation of yours must have cost. There's just not enough money for that. At least not for everyone. So people with more money would be privileged in terms of their lifespan. And people don't want that.

Max can't think of anything to counter that right now.

Anyway, says Antoine, I also saw your interview. That woman is a stupid nitwit if ever I saw one. Anyway, I've decided that I'll help you with your search. That's why I wanted to be alone with you for a while.

Max suddenly asks: will you come with me to Spain? Antoine's eyes widen. Max has to explain. It's a logical point to start. Spain was the last place I lived.

Before I went to Mexico, I lived there. I don't know what happened to my house. I only have vague recollections, but if I left anything behind for myself, it must be there.

Spain, says Antoine. Oh dear.

You don't like travelling?

No idea, she says, never done it.

...&...

The station is dilapidated, the platforms dirty. Max and Antoine, who's standing next to him, both brought a trolley suitcase and somehow it feels nice to be travelling with her, but he's also nervous.

Then a huge passenger train, made out of steel and glass, floats into the hall. The front end has the aerodynamic shape of a futuristic spaceship from Max's time, but this behemoth sounds like an antique steam train. After coming to a halt, it sinks down a few inches in front of the platform. With even more hissing and puffing, the doors open. The conductor who steps out is wearing overalls, a mask and gloves. He has kind eyes, scans their wrists and gestures for them to get in quickly.

The compartment they enter has seats that are spaced closely together. An announcement is made through the intercom for the new passengers to be seated in their reserved seats as soon as possible.

Max is nervous. He used to be nervous back then as well, every time he travelled. Did he have his passport with him? And if so, where had he put it? Where was his ticket? Had he packed his toothbrush and brought enough knickers with him? Had he forgotten anything? His prescription drugs, his sunglasses? Did he have cash in the right currency for the taxi from the airport?

On this trip, he doesn't need a passport, ticket or cash, Ilse has arranged everything via the chip in his wrist. Now he also understands why Antoine has never been outside the district. Travelling is incredibly expensive if you don't have a good reason to do it. A holiday to Spain costs an entire year's basic income.

He searches for his seat. The uniformed man shouts for him to hurry. Antoine shows him his spot by the window. Max has to step over the legs of a woman occupying the seat next to him. Antoine sits one row ahead, also at the window.

They've hardly sat down when the train starts moving.

After only a few seconds, they shoot out of the hall and the train starts accelerating. Max is pressed into the back of his seat with a G-force he vaguely remembers from fairground rides.

Antoine, who has never been on a hover train before, lets out a small shriek of enthusiasm. The people in front of her look back amused. The pressure decreases slightly after the train reaches speed and Max can breathe normally again. Out of the city, into the great wide open.

The landscape flashes past them. No vast pastures or vistas to relax the eyes, no, everything is forest, small pieces of land, lakes, canals, ditches, houses, greenhouses and small crop fields. Because of the speed, which Antoine tells him is over 450 miles per hour, he can barely see anything at all. Before he can focus on something, it's already far behind him. If the landscape opens up briefly and a quick glimpse shows the silhouette of a city on the horizon, it's soon obscured again by the patchwork of woods, fields and roads, a slide show that moves by so fast it makes Max dizzy.

So he just looks at the screen in front of him, which shows a few people in a strange setting. He tries to guess what it's about, which isn't easy without sound. It's probably a quiz. He always used to know all the answers, but now he doesn't even want to try.

Aren't you Mr Flowerday? the woman next to him asks. She's about his age. Neatly dressed in a tight, beige suit with a high black turtleneck.

Manicured hands, some understated pieces of jewellery around her neck and wrists. There's a screen on the small table in front of her. On it, Max sees a complicated spreadsheet. Her opening line makes it sound like she lives in his building, but she says she recognizes him from the broadcast on The Net. His interview was watched by a lot of people, not only in his own department.

No, says Max, but apparently, I look a bit like him.

I could've sworn it was you, says the woman.

I saw that freak show too, he says, it sounds like a weird story to me. Someone who has himself put into a coma for a hundred years and then gives a loudmouthed interview. Talking about history and how important it is.

The woman hesitates for a moment but then it turns out she also has an opinion on the interview.

Well, part of me understands that you would want to know what happened if you came from somewhere in the early 21st century. Gee, what a time that must have been, when nobody knew what was coming, when everyone was living it up like there was no tomorrow.

Max's jaw drops. For a moment, he regrets pretending to be someone else, but before that regret grows, the woman says: he was a bit of a freak though yeah, that man, a weirdo indeed. He spoke quite incoherently and something probably went wrong with his brain during that coma.

Yes, says Max, the guy was not quite right in the head if you ask me. He stays quiet after that and when the woman also remains silent, he quickly puts in an earpiece that gives him sound to accompany the images on his screen. Ideally, he would like to dissolve into nothingness for a while. Attach himself to one of the thousands of images that shoot by every minute or teleport into the quiz show he can now hear, even though he doesn't understand the questions, let alone know the answers.

Max, shouts Antoine, because the earpieces also adequately eliminate external sounds or automatically compensate for them. We'll be in Brussels in five minutes, she says.

2125 - THE HIBERNATOR

Caught off guard, Max looks at the woman next to him, but by now she too is wearing earpieces and so won't have heard his name.

...&...

It's late by the time the boat arrives. Dusk has started to fall, a much faster process here than in the North, Max recalls. The island's capital has been better preserved than his own city. The town planners have been less rigorous here. The city center with its stately buildings, galleries and pavement cafes is still almost exactly as he remembers it. He loves walking through the old streets, even though the roads have been replaced by green spaces, there are no cars and almost all transport is taking place underground.

A huge experience center with seven floors above and nine floors below ground level has replaced the big department stores. There are artisanal workshops where you can have things custom-made. Clothes to your own design, furniture made to order in the sizes you want, jewellery, shoes, in fact you can have anything made here.

He misses the old smells. The salty sea air, mixed with petrol and diesel stench, the smoke from wood-burning stoves, the food smells of street barbecues, garlic, fish, chorizo and other tapas. And the characteristic sounds of the past as well, with screaming people and children, sputtering scooters, sirens and roaring buses. Everything here is so very quiet.

Antoine can't stop looking around. Enthusiastically, she narrates everything she sees, much to the annoyance of Max, who keeps saying: yeah, I see it too.

Their hotel is in the city center on an upscale street along the river that, in this spring season, is filled to the brim with rainwater rushing down from the mountains to the sea. Max remembers that usually, over the course of the summer, it would run completely dry.

He makes a beeline for the bar and orders a Cuba libre, then is surprised that the bartender puts it in front of him without asking any questions. The slightly syrupy coke, softened by the oily, brown rum they seem to be distilling here on the island these days. The drink doesn't really resemble the rum and coke of old, but the flavour still manages to invoke his nostalgic feelings for a while. He takes a few sips and asks the guy behind the bar for an extra shot of rum. Or is it a girl? Max does like androgynous people, they're much, much more prevalent now than they used to be.

Max asks how the person wants to be addressed.

Doesn't matter to me, he or she says cheerfully. Max settles on boy for now.

Antoine and the boy look at each other for a moment and there seems to be a spark, but it could also be Max's imagination.

A while later in the lounge, with another double rum, Max asks Antoine whether she's lesbian or bisexual. Or straight after all? Antoine takes a breath and dives in.

We don't put people in boxes that way, she says. What does it matter where your sexual preferences lie? Many people no longer have a preference and make out with all genders, what you used to call bisexual. It's about liking someone very much, so much that you want to be intimate with him, her or them. Nobody just sleeps around, and not only because there's big risks involved with that.

Big risks? asks Max, you mean STIs like AIDS?

AIDS? Don't know that. Is that an illness from your time? Antoine smiles vaguely.

Max thinks that smile is meant for him, but looking over his shoulder, he sees the boy who served them sitting further down at the bar. He's apparently done working. The boy raises his glass for a moment and Max answers his greeting with a nod.

He turns back to Antoine, who continues her story: Well, it's been replaced by some other beauties then. Not just deadly ones, but also one that led to male infertility, which has been a huge pandemic.

Hah, I've been saying that for ages, says Max cheerfully. Nature itself regulates overpopulation. Max feels bigger for a moment, the Doomsday Professor scores one for the team.

He wants to know what happened to lust then. With the pure, animalistic primal urge of men and women to have sex with each other.

Sex just for the sake of sex is something you do alone, there are devices and tools that can help you with that, says Antoine.

Devices, tools? Max exclaims, startled. He doesn't want to hear about it. Awkward. Sex with devices? Where has all the romance gone? he sighs.

Antoine laughs.

Of course there's romance, Antoine says dreamily. People still flirt, people still long for one another, poems are still written and songs are still made about love and sadness. If you like someone, you still date them. Anything can happen, but it takes time to get familiar enough with each other to get intimate. Max takes another sip of his rum and coke. He feels the effect of the alcohol slowly creeping up, as if the brown liquid is creeping through his veins and branching out to his nerves and muscles.

It also feels like someone's slowly tightening a vice around his stomach. In addition, he has a stabbing headache that keeps returning ever since the train journey.

I'm not doing so well, Max says.

Antoine looks a little crestfallen.

Let's go to my village tomorrow, he says.

They walk towards the lift. Antoine wants to support Max as he cringes in pain, but he pushes her away.

I can see myself up, he says irritated. Don't worry. You hurry back to the bar to flirt with that cute boy.

...&...

They have a chauffeured car, a large off-road vehicle with deep treads, a gaudy light blue colour and room for at least seven people. The driver tells Max he knows his village and thinks he knows where the house he describes is located. Max had hoped for someone who could also tell him a bit more about his island. Taxi drivers always know everything. Max discovered that the Spanish language is still hidden somewhere in his brain, complete with all its thirteen tenses, irregularities and incomprehensible grammar. He speaks it fluently, but unfortunately, he's the only one speaking. The driver's only words since they left have been 'si' and 'no'.

After crossing the last hill, he sees his village. It's not much bigger than it used to be and its two churches still stick out above the pattern of stone houses like the tiers of a grotesque wedding cake.

As they get closer, he does see some differences. Many village houses have disappeared. There are trees everywhere, along the road, in the village, at all edges of the fields, an endless number of trees with low vegetation surrounding them.

Trees, trees, trees, says Antoine out of nowhere, the Trillion Tree Campaign they came up with last century. And then they just started planting. Globally, we are even close to two trillion trees by now. The earth is slowly cooling down, she adds. Simple, isn't it? Antoine leans against the back seat, groggy after a night of partying with the bartender.

They went out on the town, as she puts it: to visit obscure pubs and dance venues that were open until dawn.

Max is on the edge of his seat though. He knows the way and enthusiastically indicates to the driver where to turn left and right, until they reach the road to his former home. He recognizes the curves, the rolling hills and valleys and feels his heartbeat speeding up.

He has been up and down this lane here a thousand times, by car, by bike, on foot. The gravel has been replaced by a faded green, solid substance, the kind of synthetic material that is used for road surfaces these days. The farms that originally stood along this road have disappeared or have been replaced by smaller wooden or printed houses, surrounded by small crop fields. Long before they reach the gate, Max sees the spot where his house used to be. The two pillars that flank the gate are still authentic. Even the stone lions on top are still in place, albeit half weathered and crumbling. The gate opens electrically after the driver honks his horn.

He stands in front of his house. At least, in front of its replacement. The original stone villa has been replaced by a printed building.

It still has roughly the same shape, two classic fincas with their backs to each other, connected by a glass middle section.

The garden, where Felice laid out the beginnings of something like an edible forest garden in his time, has turned into an oasis of greenery, an endless variety of shrubs, vines and other plants can still be seen under the trees. Even the pond he dug is still there, an oasis of aquatic plants, reeds and giant lilies.

A young woman approaches. Blonde curls, Asian eyes, dark skin. She is maybe 30, wearing some kind of dungarees and a white, dirty shirt. She has a broad smile. Not so many grouches left, Max thinks. Even the si and no driver had a broad grin on his face the whole trip. A trillion smiles, could that be a plan as well?

Hello, welcome to Villa Felice, my name is Fleur. Her English diction is beautiful, though Max does hear the accent of another language in it. She wants to know how she can be of service to them.

Ricci, Felice Ricci, says Max, a strange thrill went through him just now when this unknown girl mentioned Felice's name. He looks at an olive tree he had planted himself.

That tree is more than a hundred years old, he says.

Indeed, says the girl, somewhat surprised at Max's pronunciation of the full name.

Indeed, Felice Ricci lived here a hundred years ago. Hero worship has gone out of fashion, but we're still proud that our villa bears her name.

Yep, says Max, I know all about it. And this house is a shelter for political refugees now, right?

Fleur just keeps smiling. It used to be, yes. Now it's a retreat for the Global Thinkers Society.

Really? asks Antoine. Her hangover seems to have vanished into thin air.

Oh, and what's that? asks Max and he slaps his hand on his heart, my name is Max Flowerday. If you're somewhat familiar with the history...

Are you related to Felice? says Fleur excitedly, without answering the question. Her husband's name was also Max Flowerday. Great. May I show you around? Gosh, this is very special. She gestures for them to follow her, turns and leads them up the driveway to the house.

There have been some changes to the layout, Max notes. This is where the dining room used to be and the stairs to the first floor were over there, he says to no one in particular.

Gosh, says Fleur, you don't look that old, haha. It's been this way for at least 70 years. The original building collapsed and was rebuilt in the 2050s.

He is 158, says Antoine.

Fleur ignores or doesn't hear that comment. Max walks to the terrace which still offers panoramic views of the region. You can see for six miles or more across the hills. In front of them lies the village and behind it forests, trees and more forests.

Max says he needs to sit down for a minute and takes a seat on a bench overlooking the landscape.

Fleur asks if he wants a drink.

A glass of water, please. He looks out over the garden and fondly remembers the peace he always found here.

Fleur brings him the water and sits down next to him.

Global Thinkers, what are they? he asks her.

It's kind of like a think tank of critical scientists.

Max perks up.

Interesting. Are you a member?

No way, her smile turns into a laugh for a moment. You should think of this as a kind of guest house that members of the Society can book, I am one of the managers.

I take care of breakfast and lunch and my partner arranges dinner. Together, we take care of the house, the garden, the forest and the animals. Members come to this place to talk to each other about all kinds of topics. It's a home for philosophers, economists and all kinds of -logists.

Historians too? Max asks hopefully.

Antoine cannot suppress a smile.

Fleur looks confused at first, thinks about it and then says decidedly: No, they no longer exist.

That's what you think, says Antoine.

Fleur's partner walks onto the terrace. She puts her hand to her mouth and lets out a small shriek.

Mr. Max Flowerday, she calls out. Oh my, it really *is* you.

Max is confused, as are Fleur and Antoine. He looks at the woman intently. She is slightly broader than Fleur, also has blonde curls, but bright blue eyes, Balkan or Polish heritage. Max figures she must have seen his hopeless performance on The Net.

This is the man I told you about, Maria tells Fleur. Max, the husband of Felice Ricci, the man who spent a hundred years in a coma.

Fleur now jumps up as if she were sitting next to a patient with an infectious disease. She looks at him with open mouth.

Maria steps forward and hugs Max. She has tears in her eyes and her voice cracks.

I have been hoping you would come.

...&...

Max studies what's on his plate: a grilled slice of watermelon, deep-fried yam potato, something like broccoli stems covered in sticky slices of garlic and red chilli rings, and a grilled cauliflower steak in the middle. He thinks of steak with french fries and Belgian mayonnaise, but once he starts eating, he marvels at the unusual sweet, sour and salty flavors battling to get the upper hand in his mouth.

Maria and Fleur both anxiously watch everything Max does. They just can't believe their eyes. This man lived here a hundred years ago, started the foundation that manages this house, he is none other than Felice Ricci's husband. Antoine looks at it all with amusement, she is visibly enjoying the meal that has been served to her.

A man sits across from Max. He is tall, broad but the most notable characteristic is his age. Max estimates him to be around a hundred years old but it could just as easily be more. He's very relaxed and visibly enjoying his meal. With every bite he takes, he closes his eyes to savor it for a moment, as if he has never tasted anything so delicious. Maria explained that it's actually a changeover day, that new guests will arrive tomorrow. But Leonardo de Vries missed his boat, he's not leaving until the next morning.

On purpose, he says in Dutch. I just didn't feel like going home yet. It's way too nice here with these girls around, Leonardo says and chuckles.

2125 - THE HIBERNATOR

Fleur looks at him questioningly because she doesn't understand him. Max looks surprised as Leonardo addresses him in his own language.

I live near you, he says, as he catches Max's glance. He introduces himself as the only member of the Society who hasn't studied.

Self-taught student of life, one hundred years old, philosopher without a degree, yet appreciated by academics, anarchist with a profound dislike of schools and universities, he adds to his introduction. Nice to meet you here, Mr. Flowerday. I have already heard your strange history.

Call me Max, says Max.

Okay Max, says Leonardo and thinks for a moment. We're old enough to call each other by our first names. What, he then asks, is your opinion on the state of the world as you found it after a hundred-year hiatus?

Huh? asks Max. Where to start? Although it was meant mostly rhetorically, Leonardo helps him out.

What struck you the most?

Many answers shoot through Max's mind. Such as that technology has made little progress, that prosperity really hasn't risen much, that growth has come to an end, that there is little world news, that the world isn't very sexy anymore, but in the end he comes back to his pet subject and says: What struck me most is that the past no longer matters. I find that the most striking and also most irritating. Of course, that's partly because I'm a historian but you, as a philosopher of the older generation, must see the problem with that as well.

Oh, not really, says Leonardo. As a matter of fact, I quite enjoy it. Besides, not all history has disappeared. What would philosophy be without Nietzsche and Kant, without Marcus Aurelius, Plato, Socrates? Or even without Jesus Christ or the prophet Muhammad? No, no, it's absolutely not true that the entire history of mankind has been erased.

Yeah, no, says Max. I did hear that art history still exists, and perhaps philosophers will also draw on the ideas of classical thinkers, but isn't it true that humanity has been able to evolve throughout time because of the mistakes people made before them?

Ah, says Leonardo. A broad smile appears on his wrinkled face. It's just your professional curiosity that leads you to this opinion. You're just curious about all the things that happened during your absence. I just did a quick search for you on The Net, you're the Doomsday Professor aren't you? And now I suppose you want to hear which of your dark predictions came to pass? He laughs loudly while he says it. You rose from the dead to prove yourself right?

Leonardo starts dabbing up the liquid left on his plate with a piece of bread and puts it in his mouth. With his mouth full, he just keeps talking. Rest assured, the events will have been written down somewhere. But for now, history is a pretty closed book.

That sounds very appropriate indeed, Max grunts. And that's perhaps also part of the problem, that people are kept ignorant. That was also common during the industrial revolution. Keep people ignorant of your real intentions as a ruler. First through religion, then through sports, games, television. And when, about 120 years ago, none of that sufficed anymore, serious news coverage was buried under a flood of nonsense on the Internet, that's how we got even dumber. So now no one should know where this new, present world came from?

Leonardo looks at him jovially; he seems unimpressed by Max's arguments.

Recent history, he says, from the 2030s to the 2070s, has been quite traumatic for everyone of my generation.

Young people, born after 2075, are only vaguely aware of what their parents have had to go through. The crises they went through. What would you like to know about all that? And why would we want to keep dwelling on all that misery when we have found a solution? It's over, Mr. Flowerday. And now we're focusing on the future again.

Well, says Max, what interests me, for example, is how we turned the tide. What or who saved the world? Which leaders saved humanity from destruction? Where are those heroes?

Heroes, messiahs, leaders, dictators, we're quite done with them all, you must have noticed that by now. Like the days of democracy, socialism, capitalism that are also far behind us, Leonardo continues. There is no more hero worship, Max. It's too old-fashioned. Gone are all those statues, street names, monuments. All nonsense, the past will only drag us down.

Hence Villa Felice, Max notes snidely. Leo laughs. The exception that proves the rule, eh? he retorts.

You yourself laid down that name in the statutes of the foundation, Fleur interrupts.

Maria looks a little crestfallen at Leonardo. She seems to want to say something about her heroine, but instead, she bites her tongue, along with the last of the vegetables from her plate. Max is also silent for a moment. He wonders about his own motives. Does he indeed still want to be vindicated? To be able to say: I told you so a hundred years ago? Totally useless because no one to whom he could say that is still alive.

Isn't unhappiness necessary to be happy? he wonders aloud. Don't we appreciate the sun because sometimes the clouds hide it and rain down on us? Don't we feel liberated only after we have first experienced captivity?

Ha ha, you should have been a preacher, Max. Leonardo's roaring laughter fills the veranda from front to back.

Antoine and the two managers of Villa Felice listen with bated breath to the dialogue, which Max and Leonardo are conducting in English as a courtesy to their hosts.

Happiness, Leonardo says, also has a different definition these days, just like freedom and bad weather. Happiness is connected to material possessions less and less, and you could also consider it a freedom that people no longer have to think about the past.

...&...

Max is up early. As is Leonardo. The previous night had been a late one, so Fleur and Maria prepared beds for Max and Antoine, so they didn't have to return to the island's capital.

They sit on the front terrace and watch the dew slowly evaporate from the plants in front of them. Max thinks of the times he used to sit here with Felice. The view was different each and every morning. Sky, mist, the red colors of dawn, cloud banks, there was always something that made the view different, never boring.

I'm actually here to find out what happened to Felice, Max says.

Leonardo looks at him, then casts a glance into his coffee cup and chuckles a bit, as he did frequently the night before. A cynical cackle that makes Max insecure, but at the same time starts to amuse him.

So you think you'll find some clue about the greatest mystery of the last century out here?

Leonardo moves his hands in the air as if sketching a huge billboard. Where has Felice Ricci gone?

Yeah, it was quite a big case, at least until 2025, says Max, looking at Leonardo's imaginary billboard.

Oh, but it got even bigger after that. Especially when your son was also kidnapped. What was his name again?

Daan, Daan Flowerday. Daan was kidnapped as well? Max is clearly shocked, another revelation.

Certainly, after all, he ran the foundation that all of you set up to control the patent on Felice's invention. That's what it was all about in the end, right? But that abduction backfired. And the losers they arrested were tight-lipped about who had hired them and whether they'd also had anything to do with Felice's abduction.

Max racks his brain with the new information. Where had he ended up with his investigation into Felice's disappearance back then? He realizes how little he had always known.

I just have to know more about this, says Max. What happened, were there any suspects? It's clear who benefitted from her disappearance.

Well, who didn't? sighs Leonardo and repeats it again: who didn't? Clearly, he finds it exhausting to talk about the matter. What's your interest in finding out, Max?

When someone you love disappears, it's worse than death, Max says. I didn't have the time to figure it out a hundred years ago, but I just want to know. Is it in my nature? My occupational tendency to reconstruct the past? Is it a feeling of guilt, as if I need to know that I wasn't to blame for her disappearance?

Leo chuckles again.

Yeah, to answer questions like that, perhaps you should just find a psychiatrist, he says.

Yeah, I've got one already, says Max. And then there's the history of the past hundred years, no one wants to tell me what actually happened. That's bizarre, isn't it?

Leo looks at him somewhat pityingly. If you're over the age of 150, yeah, I guess so. Especially when you've slept through a hundred of those years. He sighs deeply. All right, Max... brace yourself, and I'll tell you. In a nutshell. Then you'll understand why no one needs to be reminded of that anymore.

And Leo begins.

...&...

Maria had told him that the donation of the villa had been arranged through a notary's office in the capital. He's there now. The office is in a building that was already ancient a hundred years ago. It seems to have been carefully restored not too long ago. Lots of marble flooring, wooden bookcases and classic desks, which have clearly been carefully recreated.

The notary is an elegant woman who speaks English at lightning speed, a bit under her breath. Max struggles to concentrate on what she's saying, even though she has an excellent command of English grammar. She seems to speak to him with some reluctance. He's distracted by her long nails, painted bright blue. She wears a black blouse of a gossamer fabric, it looks as if the buttons have been fastened incorrectly, which is also distracting. She asked every polite question imaginable. About the trip, his health, his family and his companion Antoine.

Max complains that everything has changed on the island. All these weird new buildings, all those ugly modern cars on the road. And I miss the smell of the old days, he says. I especially miss the smell.

The notary nods understandingly but she probably has no idea what Max is talking about.

He starts to feel faint and begins breathing shallowly. Concentrate, he thinks. Concentrate, focus.

He suddenly remembers that other time he sat here, a hundred years ago. Back then, it was Francisco Álvaro de Luna sitting opposite him, a nice guy. He vividly recalls him sitting there, suddenly also recognizes the cardboard folder lying between him and this woman today. Francesca Álvaro de Luna is her name, apparently they still have little imagination when it comes to naming. The shortness of breath gets worse.

Antoine sees what is happening. She apologizes to Francesca and asks for some water for Max. Francesca, who now also sees that Max isn't doing well, rushes out of the room.

Max is squinting and he can see tiny floaters blooming at the edge of his vision. He's tired. Tired from the enervating evening with Leonardo and everything he heard that morning. Actually, he's tired of everything. Ideally, he would like to lie down under a tree and stay there forever. Maybe because he knows what's going to happen next and is stressing about the closed folder lying there in front of him on the table. Antoine stands bent over him with an arm around his shoulders. That arm suddenly feels really heavy, but also very nice.

Francesca returns with a glass of water. She asks if he's doing alright and lets out a small cough before continuing her story.

You gave your file to us back then for safekeeping, it's this folder and these boxes. Behind her, four huge archive boxes are stacked up and Max looks at them in amazement. This folder contains an envelope with a letter you wrote to yourself at the time.

A rather extensive story. It's a personal letter, in your own language; we haven't looked into it. We'll go through your business matters later. If we can help you with anything else, don't hesitate to ask. I will leave you alone for now, so you can decide what to do with all that paper. She made that last word sound a bit like she was talking about something dirty. This was probably the only paper they still kept in their safe.

Fine, Max only says, closes his eyes and hears the file folder being pushed towards him.

After a minute or two, the floaters have disappeared and he opens his eyes again. He opens the folder. He sees a handwritten letter, instantly recognizes the handwriting and, looking at the last page, sees his name, with the words 'good luck' above it.

He starts reading. Antoine, sitting next to him, tries to read along but Max shields the letter with his arm like a schoolboy not wanting a fellow pupil to cheat. Antoine shuffles back and forth nervously, it seems to take Max an eternity to finish reading, then he starts all over again.

What does it say? Antoine wants to know.

It's a letter to *me*, Max says emphatically. For me personally, Antoine.

Yeah yeah, Antoine says impatiently. But what does it say? You didn't bring me along for nothing, did you?

That letter is to me and from me, Max says crossly. He looks at the pile of boxes a little despondently.

The notary has returned. She's speaking in Spanish now and Antoine looks disappointed. She clearly doesn't understand a word of the verbal torrent flying across the table.

Max hears that in the last hundred years, the financial world has been turned upside down completely. Banks, financial markets, major shareholders, extreme wealth, all these things have disappeared one by one. Francesca's office was tasked with safely investing his capital back then but it turns out there's not much left because of all the capital gains tax that had to be paid over it every year. Max doesn't care. Just deposit it to my wrist, he jokes.

The letter to himself brought him even closer to the moment he sat here, some hundred years ago. He sees a defeated man, a man at the end of his rope, a lover obsessed with finding his beloved again, an incurably ill man who in truth just wants to do away with himself.

...&...

In the suite he has rented, the four boxes are piled up next to the sofa upon which he and Antoine are sitting. Antoine looks uneasily at all that paper, smells it and then coughs a little because of all the dust and the musty smell coming from the boxes. Max loves that smell.

You made it this far, Max had written to himself, and no further. You've had to abandon your investigation into Felice's disappearance because death awaits you. You've decided to go to sleep for a hundred years, in the hope they will fix your sick body and perhaps it will work out so you can find out what happened to Felice a hundred years from now. All the archives will surely be open now that you're reading this. Hopefully you'll be able find the answer to what happened to her then.

He doesn't want to share the melodramatic wallowing in self-pity that the rest of the letter contains with Antoine. He's ashamed of it. What he also doesn't share with Antoine is the fact that he's now starting to remember that he actually saw the whole business in Mexico as a form of euthanasia. The letter also tells him that, at the time, he didn't give himself much of a chance of surviving that coma. That he actually lost hope of ever seeing Felice alive again and therefore, even if he hadn't had an incurable disease, he would still rather be dead.

But there is still plenty he did want to share with Antoine. He reads to her. Oil companies, the automotive industry, electric utility companies, even energy suppliers that have invested in solar or wind energy, banks, shareholders, billionaires, oligarchs, all of them have a vested interest in not releasing the patent on the technology behind FreeEnergy, which was Felice's ultimate goal.

Because oil is the lifeblood of the world as it is today, the black gold that'll be worthless if FreeEnergy's patent is shared with the world.

Antoine is impressed, he sees her racking her brain, sighing deeply every now and then. The number of documents is huge, she bought a small camera which she uses to scan everything Max gives her and then she stores it somewhere on The Net.

Quite a lot of history all at once, eh? says Max. His reference is to all the smelly paper but his thoughts go to the hundred years of war, disasters and pandemics that Leonardo revealed that morning. I'm back in my element, he adds, a little redundantly given the unwavering, broad grin on his face.

When Max pauses for a moment, he looks at Antoine, who just keeps going. She has her long hair tied up in a bun, is sitting on her knees and grunts at the documents she grabs one by one, scanning them with her eyes and sometimes with her camera.

You would've been a great student in my class. Is history becoming something enjoyable yet, rather than something scary, something better erased?

I never said I don't like it, Antoine grunts, I love investigating things. I just see a lot of dead ends. And let's not forget, the perpetrators of Felice's kidnapping are all long dead. Their descendants have been impoverished by the inheritance tax, their power dissolved in the new governance form of the Union. The only place where you can still find stories about bad guys and the heroes who fight them is in the movies.

I want to find that bad guy, I want to dance on his grave, growls Max.

Does your letter provide any leads?

Sure. He points to the boxes. I hadn't been searching for nothing all those years.

...&...

They stand in front of a travel vending machine that requires spoken instructions to get a ticket for the trip to Barcelona. Antoine is excited, she has never flown before. But there were so many things she had never done before: never been abroad, never slept in a hotel, never scanned 90 pounds of paper, never even eaten oysters, which are widely available on the island.

Max thought the boat trip over had been a disaster so he had now opted for flying.

As soon as Max exits the terminal, he regrets that decision. He sees a huge cigar, 500 feet long, with a cabin underneath that resembles something like an aeroplane without nose, tail or wings.

Antoine beams at the sight of the zeppelin. She talks non-stop about the airship's technology, which she's had her guide delve into. This thing is going to take her to an altitude of close to 10,000 feet, and she has never been that high either. It'll take them to Barcelona in under two hours.

Aeroplanes are rare, only used sporadically, she says. Hydrogen-powered zeppelins are the alternative.

In the cabin, Antoine immediately sits down by the window, while Max goes in search of a seat where he doesn't have to look outside. The cabin shakes as if there's severe turbulence, although they haven't even left yet. Next to him, a man reassures him. No zeppelin has ever crashed. Not once. Yes, that's easy if you erase the history of Graf Ferdinand von Zeppelin along with everything else, says Max. The man looks at him in amazement.

2125 - THE HIBERNATOR

On the hover train in Barcelona, they sit down in the spacious first-class seats. A woman sits opposite them. She's in her mid-forties and wears a suit of light beige fabric that looks like wool but isn't, it fits perfectly. Her dark brown eyes stand out brightly against her light skin and blonde hair. The eyes that stare at him for a moment before they refocus on a glass screen folded up from her chair, are not unfriendly. The screen is somewhat transparent, and Max thinks he can see a film, with people in tight suits in a spaceship. He never used to like these kinds of films much. You didn't usually see a slow zeppelin in there; a hover train was also old-fashioned.

A hundred years ago, Max starts telling Antoine, they really thought that by this time the whole world would be a computerized robot society. In which people wouldn't be doing much more than occasionally repairing flying taxis. And where all food would come in tubes, no more need for agriculture. Electricity would come from mega-power plants powered by futuristic fuel cores. Travelling would be done with capsules, shot through tubes at rocket speed, connecting major cities around the world. A small part of society would be very content and the majority, the rabble, would live outside the walled cities and feed themselves on the rubbish thrown over the wall. There would also always be resistance fighters, mostly living underground in the sewers and fighting for the freedom of mankind, against the dictators and oligarchs. I haven't seen anything resembling resistance here yet. Of course, the distribution of wealth has been quite successful, but a little revolution would certainly liven things up a bit.

Maybe we Protestants could be seen as something of a resistance movement?

Really? So what do you guys do? Protesting in the streets, blocking traffic? Do you have guns and are you going to seize power?

Max sees the woman opposite him listening.

No, we don't impose our will on others. It's about a state of mind we're in and we want space for that. It's not a matter of enforcing anything, it's a matter of taking space. Most of that happens in your mind, sometimes what we want clashes with the authorities, then we use passive resistance.

Doesn't really sound like a resistance movement, Max grumbles. The Protestants are just kids who want to oppose something, no matter what, the woman across from them suddenly says. They're just a group of bored youths.

A silence ensues. Antoine looks at her with a cynical expression.

Such opinions also don't mean anything to us. Maybe we are indeed children. But if being an adult means being like you, then that's all the reason we need for not wanting to become one.

Ouch, burn, Max says and grins. He looks the woman straight in the eye for a moment. Her expression is rather cheeky and she grins a little as if to say she isn't sorry for interfering with their conversation.

You're Max Flowerday, aren't you? she asks. The one from the hundred-year-coma.

Sorry, do I know you? Max asks with a slight mocking tone. No, says the woman, and I don't know you either. But I did see that broadcast. Madeleine. Madeleine Verdun, nice to meet you. We're from the same city. She pats her hand on her heart and takes a slight bow.

Okay, so I don't have to introduce myself anymore, Max says dryly. Sorry to drop in on your conversation like this, she continues. This film really sucks, she says and pushes the screen towards her armrest, into which it disappears automatically.

Max isn't sure if he wants to continue the conversation with her but still can't resist getting his point across.

There hasn't been a single moment in history when there was no movement opposing the ruling power. By standing out from the crowd, by speaking up or by fighting the power either peacefully or forcefully. Maybe it's just that you don't know. That there is resistance, but you just don't know where it is and who they are.

You're a funny man, Max, says Madeleine. There's both pity and mockery in her voice. Perhaps you're the resistance. All by yourself, the one-man-resistance movement against the Peoples' Union. But what are you resisting?

Max looks out of the window. He has a strange feeling about this woman. Uncanny, weird, he can't think of the exact word for it just now. She is pretty, looks well-groomed and she isn't unfriendly either, but she's hugely annoying.

She leans over and puts her hand on Max's thigh. He looks at it with amazement. It's a beautiful, slender hand, its nails are painted in an inconspicuous colour. He looks at her a little startled by this sudden intimacy when she whispers in her soft voice: Sorry Max, I can be a terrible jerk sometimes.

...&...

Home again. Max is tired from the journey. The boxes with the documents were left behind, but the chaos of scanned documents gave him his first sleepless night.

Ilse, can I request another guide if I'm not satisfied with you? he asks. He sits in his study and stares at the desk surface on which Ilse now appears. It's raining so hard outside that the downpour deprives him of his view of the outside world.

Aren't you satisfied, Max? No.

What's the problem?

You don't know enough about the things I'm looking for. I've been told I need to train you better if I want more from you. But I think I would prefer a different guide then, one that's more capable of doing things by herself.

It doesn't work that way, Max. I think you don't understand the concept. I'm nothing more than a parallel dimension, a mirror of yourself. You can rename a guide, remake their image, but he or she will be no different from me or from you.

So I'm stuck with you?

I wouldn't say that.

I really want to know everything that happened in the past and you say there's no information about that. Antoine scanned thousands of documents but I'm not getting anything back from you. You've got to give me something.

What do you want me to do with the documents?

How the hell should I know, read them, store them, study them, index them, isn't that what guides do?

They do if you ask them, yes, but you have explicitly indicated that you don't appreciate any own initiative.

He sees that his avatar has a smile on her lips.

Surely the machine won't have a sense of humor as well? he thinks.

It's quiet for a few seconds, then Ilse reports that she has studied and indexed the documents. She lists the categories and Max wonders if his comments about Ilse's behaviour have already affected her. After all, she's a being that in a matter of seconds can think more deeply, know more and work faster than he could in four weeks. He would've spent months on those scans.

I want to know what my documents say about Felice's disappearance, Max says.

Ilse replies: On Wednesday 18 October 2023, she was last seen getting into a limousine, together with her personal assistant Alfred Dillam. This happened at the entrance of the Paramount Hotel Dubai where she was staying. The limousine was not ordered by them and, according to your notes, it's a mystery why she got in. The day before, she had a conversation with a certain John Brederoo the second, who stated he didn't know anything at the time.

Dillam never resurfaced either?

I don't know.

I don't think a guide should say something like that. Interpol was looking for Felice, right? Max recalls. Can't you find anything about that?

It's quiet for a moment. Computer time, Max thinks, and in his mind he hears a hard drive spinning the way it used to sound.

Interpol no longer exists, says Ilse.

So what's the name of its successor? International police? Peoples' Union Investigation?

Union Police Force, says Ilse. But their computers, of course, are secret.

But archives older than 75 years should be public, right? They have to be public, Max says a little desperately. Find out where they keep them. And don't give me that DataFade talk again. Many old archives must still exist.

Again, he hears that hard drive in his mind. Again, more time than Ilse normally needs.

I've got them, says Ilse.

Ilse starts summarising with tremendous speed, Max listens to the account with bated breath. The text comes from a police report written by a certain Jonathan Christianni.

Felice and Alfred were in Dubai, Ilse recounts. The conversation with John Brederoo took place at his huge beachfront villa. His father was the CEO of Global Energy, a conglomerate of energy companies. There were allegations that GE hindered, delayed and sabotaged research into FreeEnergy and other alternative energy sources.

Keep going, Max says.

Well, the next day they were met by a limousine, Ilse says. Dillam stated afterwards that they were convinced that they were getting into Brederoo's car. Pretty soon, their eyes got blurry and eventually they lost consciousness.

Alfred woke up in a 10-by-6-foot cell. He suspects his food was drugged. Later on, he also received injections in his arm. His cell seemed to turn into a palace. The drugs felt amazing. After a while, he couldn't remember his name. The weeks became months, months became years or maybe they didn't. Somewhere along the line, he gave up. In exchange for a hefty sum of money and his release, and after a series of death threats, he promised to keep quiet about his abduction.

2125 - THE HIBERNATOR

So that's all in that police report of... Max blinks his eyes, tries to process the information, but sinks back exhausted in his desk chair.

Of Jonathan Christianni, Ilse helps him. Let me continue, are you still listening? Dillam did not see Felice after they got into the car. Never again, it literally says here, Ilse says coldly. A moment of silence again before she continues: Jonathan Christianni is featured in the Story Institute.

What's that then? sighs Max.

A place you need to go to in person, Ilse replies, and there seems to be irritation in her voice.

Could she really get angry?

...&...

It's an imposing building. Probably about eighty years old, as there is no wood anywhere in sight. Concrete, aluminum, glass and natural stone only. The entrance is spacious and looks like the portal of a classical cathedral. Wide stairs and high doors. To Max, it looks almost like a building from the Third Reich.

Max follows a girl assigned to him by the doorman, who sits behind a raised counter like a king on his throne. He monitors all incoming and outgoing traffic and guests who report to him get paired up with one of his errand girls and boys.

The words National Archives are chiseled into the marble blocks above the entrance, but that name is no longer correct. Story Institute, reads the visitor's badge that appears in his lenses.

Only five branches exist in the world. This is where stories are kept. Narratives of thousands of people, recorded after the DataFade. A private initiative by a group of people who wanted to go back to the lore of the land by telling stories from generation to generation. At first, they did it the very old-fashioned way, because there was a huge animosity against all zeros and ones after the war. Shot with 3D cameras on old-fashioned celluloid. After a decade or so, they did go back to digitizing the films, storing them on servers that weren't connected to The Net and inaccessible to anyone that couldn't be bothered to come in person.

They enter a room with a large number of viewing cabins. Max looks at them with a mixture of awe and fear. They're arranged in rows, three layers above each other, like carts in a fairground ride or a cable car. As he follows the girl up the stairs, he feels his breath quicken. On the top floor, they pass cabins with people lying in them. He can't see what they're looking at, but lights are flickering inside the cabins.

At the end of the row, there's a vacant box and the girl unlocks it by swiping her wrist past the door. Max takes a seat inside.

He sees nothing there, no screen, no image, there's only an empty tabletop in front of him. When the girl wants to turn and leave, he looks at her, startled.

I don't know how this works, he whispers.

She stops, smiles kindly and explains to him that a guide will come and explain everything to him shortly. Then she shuts the door and waves briefly at him through the window. She doesn't notice the colour draining from Max's face.

There's dead silence in the capsule. He doesn't even hear his own breathing, but that could be because he's holding it in. When he clears his throat, the sound seems to come from outside the cabin. Instinctively, he looks at the door handle, grabs it and opens the door. The girl returns. She asks if he's done already.

No? You do need to keep the door closed, otherwise it won't work. Just be patient.

I just wanted to make sure I could get out, Max says, somewhat shaken. I'm a bit claustrophobic.

The girl looks at him with compassion but opens her hands in a gesture saying: what do you want me to do about it?

Max pulls the door shut again and tells himself that he couldn't really have been conscious at any time during his stay in the Coma Superviviente capsule, in which he stayed for a hundred years. Perhaps subconsciously then? He presses his nose to the window to see if he can see the person in the box next to him. He can't.

Hello, he calls out. Is anyone there?

The light goes out and a 3D projection of a person appears in front of him on the tabletop. The figure is a lot smaller than Max but looks straight at him. It's an older man in a white suit. With his long, grey beard, he looks a bit like God, as he used to be depicted on prayer cards.

I'm your guide, the man says kindly. I can explain what the Story Institute is if you're unfamiliar with it.

I know, you're about traditional lore. Telling stories and all that.

The projection flashes and jumps.

You can press the button in front of you once if you don't require any further explanation.

This guide appears rigid to Max. Very different from Ilse, who talks and moves smoothly and uses almost no standard answers. He presses the only button he sees in front of him.

Right, says Max. I'm looking for a certain Jonathan Christianni. Apparently, he's telling stories here.

The man disappears completely for a moment. When he returns, he freezes for a moment and then starts moving slowly back and forth. This wasn't a response to Max's question, as it turns out, but just a glitch.

The guide disappears and another person appears in front of him. More in the 3D style he is familiar with from the old days. The recording is from 2065, at least 60 years old.

My name is Jonathan Christianni, the man begins. I'm a retired Chief Superintendent from Interpol, missing persons department. I've been assigned to lead the reopened investigation into the disappearance of Felice Ricci in 2027. Since most of the files were lost because of the DataFade during the war, I'm here to record my story for posterity.

Max looks at the man's projection with amazement.

Jonathan clears his throat and looks straight into Max's eyes as if he's addressing Max personally.

I don't know who'll hear this story. Many people are interested in the Ricci mystery, the woman who disappeared in the year 2023 and for whom the whole world has been searching. I'm telling this story for those people. But I'll start with a spoiler. It's now 2065 and I continued the investigation for another three years after I retired. In the end, I had to give up. I've never been able to find out the truth about the disappearance.

Max looks tensely at the picture in front of him. He wishes he could interrupt Jonathan, ask questions, but he understands that this is not an interactive medium. This is the very oldest form of communication, just sending.

Jonathan continues. He explains that Alfred Dillam, who disappeared along with Felice, turned up in London at one point. This happened in the year 2027.

Dillam was severely addicted to heroin, a junkie, making a living by begging and shoplifting, the Chief Superintendent says. Until he was arrested for armed robbery. While going through forced withdrawal, he confessed to living under a false identity. He'd been locked up for eight months and had then been dumped as an unimportant pawn.

By now, he'd become heavily addicted though, and the money his captors had given him enabled him to support his habit for a while. He was extremely embarrassed and also too afraid to get back in touch with any old acquaintances. He decided to stay under the radar - his addiction hardly left him any other choice.

Jonathan continues with Interpol's interrogations of Dillam, in which he told them where he had last seen Felice. That was in Dubai, in the limousine that picked them up from the hotel.

Max remembers saying goodbye to her two days prior.

Dillam described his cell, how they'd gotten him addicted, first through food and later with injections. He hadn't seen or heard anything more from Felice and he knew nothing further about his guards, the location of the prison, nothing at all. His masked interrogators were really only interested in the FreeEnergy patent but, as Felice's personal assistant, he knew nothing about that.

When Jonathan is done speaking, his projection stops abruptly. Max takes a deep breath, presses the button, calls for the guide. After Max called out a few times, he finally appears.

I am your guide, he says again. I can explain what the Story Institute is if you're unfamiliar with it.

...&...

Max walks through the city. He walks through the city a lot. He remembers the time when it was fashionable to take ten thousand steps a day. At the time, he hated it because of the time it took. And because of all the people he met along the way who were eager for a chat, or whom he knew and had to, but did not want to, greet.

These days, those ten thousand steps are what get him out of bed in the mornings. For one hundred years, he hadn't moved a muscle and now he intends to make up for it as best he can. His muscles are slowly building up again and he starts to feel ever more human, more comfortable in his own skin, the colour is slowly returning to his cheeks.

He likes to walk through the neighbourhood he grew up in and where his childhood home stood, there's now a small park with a bird sanctuary on that spot. He recognizes few of the buildings that remain, but somehow he still feels at home here. Maybe it's the pattern of the streets that is still familiar, or the few houses that did survive. The atmosphere, that could be it as well. He can point out where the grocery shop, the bakery and the sex shop used to be. The factory where his father used to work has become an apartment building. The working-class neighbourhood was gentrifying even then and now it's a hodgepodge of new construction, green spaces and remnants of the old town.

He tries to avoid going back to his childhood memories. He had a domineering father prone to violence and a mother who looked for solace outside the marriage, mainly in the arms of other men. The excessive interest in history books he had as a little boy also made him unpopular with the other kids, he considered most of the girls he knew to be silly brats who made his life miserable with their bullying.

He laughed to himself for a moment. Hadn't he also erased his own past? The history with his parents? He had left his past behind when he moved out and had never really gone back to see them. Even after he had kids and they had wanted to know about their grandfather and grandmother, he referred them to Felice's parents, who lived in Italy and who they visited once every three years. By the time Sam and Daan were old enough to wonder if Max really didn't have a father and mother, his mother had already run off with one of her lovers and his father had drunk himself to death.

He's almost back home again when he crashes into someone. This isn't surprising, as he always walks hunched over and most of the time he stares at the ground, meditatively, in thought.

That's a coincidence, the woman exclaims.

Max looks at her startled, doesn't recognize her, says sorry and makes to walk on.

Madeleine, she exclaims. Madeleine Verdun, we met on the train from Spain. Remember?

Met? He thinks that's overstating it a bit but doesn't say so. Madeleine puts her manicured hand on his lower arm. Max wonders why he enjoys that. He doesn't want to enjoy it at all; he would rather keep his distance, as everyone does these days. Why is she doing this? He looks at the hand and barely hears what she says.

He does hear her say that she's been thinking about him a lot since they met on the train. It surprises him. He mutters a bit, nods and says 'yeah' a few times. When the conversation falls silent, she finally lets go of him and they face each other somewhat awkwardly.

Would you like to have dinner with me sometime? she asks.

What? Like a date or something? Max asks startled.

You know, just to enjoy some good food and a nice conversation. I'm very interested in what the world looked like a hundred years ago.

Pfff, I thought we were supposed to forget all about that.

Well, yeah, the bad parts, sure. But just, you know. You can tell me what people did back then, right? Like what they wore, what they ate, what really excited them? And, of course, what it's like to spend a hundred years in one of those capsules. Ha ha, I'm sure you never need to sleep in again.

Max doesn't want to laugh at that last comment but can't help himself.

Well okay, let's have dinner sometime, says Max. He takes her in again, from head to toe. A beautiful woman, yes, but there's something odd about her.

Well, goodbye then, he says suddenly and wants to run. That hand again, now hooked in his elbow.

Need to know how I can reach you then, Madeleine says.

Chapter 3

He waited in a small side room until the clock struck ten, then he got impatient. It looks nothing like the waiting rooms he remembers from the past. It's cosy, the space is decorated with a woman's touch, but there's also a screen to help pass the time.

Max never stopped to think that Eve also has other clients besides him. That thought bothers him now. Of course, it's her profession, but the warmth he has experienced so far during the sessions, her velvet voice, the intimacy of the conversations, they're all so unique that he can't imagine her sharing anything like that with others.

She comes to pick him up at five past ten. She wears a long, thick jumper that she pulls over her knees when she sits down. Her half-length, curly, dark hair is messy, as if she just got out of bed. Or has she been rolling around with her previous client? Max wonders, feeling a stab of jealousy.

Eve wants to know how he's doing. Did he find what he was looking for on his trip?

No, Max begins. He speaks fast and barely breathes between sentences. All of it was exhausting, the trip, the impressions, the recognition of my former hometown, I got a letter from myself, to myself. Partly because of it, I can now recall how obsessed I was back then, how much I hoped she would come back, that I would find her. Or even that she would send me a message saying she had fallen in love and found happiness with another man. I was so desperate that I would have preferred to hear that her body had been found somewhere: murdered, killed in an accident, suicide, I didn't care anymore, as long as I got an answer. It ended when I got ill, terminally ill, I feared I would die without ever finding out what had happened to her. But even then, I didn't resign myself to her disappearance, especially when I heard about that experiment in Mexico. I never believed it would succeed, at least that's what I think when I read back that letter now, I didn't necessarily want to come back. And now, here, I wonder what good it all has done. My obsession is back. I should never have been woken up.

He hears the melodrama in his own voice.

Eve looks very serious but Max suddenly feels immensely ridiculous. He wants to make a joke but can't think of anything.

Tell me something about your relationship with her, says Eve. Well... hmm, we were happily married, had two children, Daan and Sam. And we both had interesting jobs. Two scientists with smart kids.

I don't mean that. How was your relationship with her?

Max thinks. Does he feel like talking about this? What good will that do? He shrugs his shoulders. Well, of course, it wasn't always peaches and cream. I was convinced that everything she was doing was useless because the world would go to shit anyway. Ok, so maybe that message was what made me wealthy and famous, but deep down, I was really bummed that I couldn't see a way out for mankind anymore, and she could. And she was right! While I saw no future for my children and grandchildren. That it could only end in total destruction of the world. I wasn't too principled either. Ate meat, flew around the world, drove a fat petrol guzzler, I was a fatalist, pure and simple.

And Felice? asks Eve.

Felice was different, an idealist through and through; she only became more principled. She went vegan, wanted to make our house completely carbon neutral, stopped buying new stuff at one point, everything second-hand and then as little as possible. We did respect each other's work and we were a good match in bed as well. She was my great love.

And now you would like to tell her that you were wrong with your negativity? Eve wants to know.

Well, that remains to be seen. There has been a World War III, the world population was cut in half, nature struck back with climate disasters and pandemics. It's a miracle I still have any offspring. But man's resilience, eh? Indeed, I was wrong about that.

So with hindsight, you agree with her. A solution was possible after all.

Yes, but it seemed so far away. And would it have come if we hadn't screwed it all up so thoroughly first? The whole system that seemed so indestructible and unchanging had to burn down to the ground. But uhm... what are you looking for, Eve? What do you really want to know from me?

2125 - THE HIBERNATOR

You say the obsession has returned. By using that word, you're already indicating that you think it's something negative, that you need to get rid of it. You already know that you'll never find her again, and so you're obstructing your own path with an obsession that'll get you nowhere.

You might be right, he says. But do you understand that it would make a huge difference if I knew what happened to her? I also want to know who's responsible for her death.

You want revenge? asks Eve.

Perhaps, yes.

...&...

Felice walks with him on another one of his trips to Eve. She asked Max a question, but he doesn't want to answer it. He tries to get rid of her by walking faster; it doesn't work, as she speeds up as well. Even when he's almost running, she's still there by his side.

Didn't we have an argument last time I saw you? she had asked and now she hits him with another question. Didn't you threaten to leave me if I didn't stop what I was doing?

Because I thought it was dangerous. I didn't want anything to happen to you, Max says aloud. None of the people on the street look up at that because these days everyone is talking out loud into their earpiece.

Or because you couldn't handle it yourself? The fear and uncertainty. You were and still are just a scared little mouse, Maxie. You were also afraid they would throw a firebomb into the house. That they would run you or me over. Kidnap our children. You were always scared to death.

And rightly so, he snarls. Because what happened? See?

And now you're afraid of life, she says without responding to his snarl. Going to that Eve woman just to sit there and complain. An obsession? My ass. You're just afraid to move on with your life and you blame everyone else. You're no further now than you were a hundred years ago, they should've really left you in that tank, Max Flowerday.

When he gets to Eve's street, he decides to wait a few houses down. He picks a spot where he has a view of the door of Eve's practice, so he can see who's coming out.

And you're jealous too.

Out comes a handsome, ruddy-haired guy of about 30. Eve supports him as he walks onto the garden path towards a taxi just coming around the corner.

Must've had quite the electric shock to his head, Max thinks. Eve sees him and waves enthusiastically.

Caught off guard, he waves back.

Moments later, they're sitting in the garden, Eve sitting cross-legged in a big wicker chair on the lawn, with Max opposite her in another chair just like it. And there's the usual therapist question to open the conversation.

How was your week?

Am I a coward? he asks and Eve looks at him in surprise. She answers his question with one of her own, another one of those therapist clichés.

Why do you think you might be? Because Felice says so.

Then you're essentially saying it yourself, right?

No, she says I was afraid of everything that could have happened because of her work. And now she says I'm too afraid to live.

She may well be right about that.

But what is that: life? I'm a researcher, someone who uses his research about the past to explain life. Someone who works, studies, thinks. But I can't do anything in this society. There's no employment for a historian. And there's nothing to research. Everything has been arranged these days, it all seems so settled, not a ripple to disturb the sedateness of everyday life.

So, what would you have wanted differently?

You know, just a livelier environment, with problems to be solved, people getting angry and animatedly discussing laws, customs, traditions, crises. That there's something to lose or win, that there's something at stake that makes life worth living. That people debate the mistakes they made in the past. And that people who made mistakes, committed crimes, that they answer for it.

It's just boring as hell. And sex. The world has become so unsexy. My libido hasn't woken up yet after that hibernation, but shit, that's probably a good thing.

So you miss crime, sex, violence? says Eve with a slightly cynical undertone in her voice.

I miss excitement. There must be more than this, right?

But we got so much in return.

Like what?

Love, a sense of community, equality, freedom, nature restored, says Eve.

Seriously? Max says and sighs deeply. The French Revolution revisited? Liberty, equality, fraternity or death, they had that back in 1789 already.

Eve ignores his remark.

2125 - THE HIBERNATOR

There are theatres, cafes, museums, sports centers, competitions, where people can meet. In inspiration centers and community centers, people delve into spirituality and talk about the meaning of life. People take care of each other, their neighbors, their family. There is so much to do Max. As long as you're open to it and don't stay stuck in the past, your past. What's the alternative? War? Famine? Murder? Injustice?

Max looks at her wide-eyed.

Sorry, that wasn't very professional. But I mean it, Max. Find a partner, a woman you can love, because isn't that your problem? Is that what you're missing?

Well, says Max, I don't think I want that, starting all over again. I am 158. If you take into account all the time I've slept away, is there even any hope left that I'll ever find a partner?

What nonsense, Eve says fiercely. You're 58, that's nothing. I know people in their 80s starting new relationships. Many of them.

It's not about physical age. In my mind, I feel very old, worn out, a man with no mission, no purpose.

I'm just a suicide-in-disguise. My attempt failed and, as punishment, I'm back to square one. With some delay, sure, but even so.

They're both silent for a moment.

Then Eve says: you didn't really want to die Max. Anything would've been easier than that Mexican affair. You clearly weren't and aren't done living.

Max looks at her a little dazed. He managed to hold back his tears and breathes a sigh of relief that he didn't start bawling.

You need to live more in the present, enjoy the now. You're much more... more... She searches for a word. You're much more attractive than you realize.

Max thinks to himself that he hasn't actually met a woman yet with whom he would like to start a relationship. Except Eve herself, perhaps.

He considers for a moment, chuckles and then asks: Wouldn't you like to go out with me or is dating your therapist still forbidden?

Eve looks at him in astonishment. Yes, no, yes, she stutters. That's not really a taboo subject. There's more of a general rule now that in any relationship where there's a power balance, an intimate bond must be a very mutual decision. She coughs. It's not considered proper to enter into a relationship with someone over whom you have so much power that they no longer have a free choice.

Aha, says Max, so there's still hope.

Eve laughs it off.

...&...

Max walks into the restaurant and checks if his appointment is there yet. A waiter, classically dressed in a black suit, white shirt and bow tie, greets him kindly.

He guides Max to his table, which has a sign stating 'reserved' on it. He grabs it and feels it. It's made of real, thick cardstock

He used to eat out quite often but now prefers to cook at home. He finds menus too complicated these days, picks things at random and almost always accidentally chooses something he doesn't like.

This restaurant appealed to him. The name caught his eye: 'Restaurant Anno Domini 2000'. The decorations are quite retro, Venetian glassware, chrome lamps, damask on the tables and plush-covered chairs. Shiny herringbone parquet on the floor and rough stucco on the walls. He feels at home, at ease, despite all the kitsch around him.

He couldn't care less about the appointment he has here. But he had agreed to it, and even though he managed to put it off once, he could no longer delay the inevitable.

Madeleine Verdun.

He didn't see her come in, even though he's sitting at a table overlooking the entrance. She's suddenly in front of him. He stands up. That magic hand again. She rests it on the back of his hand and bends forward to plant three kisses on his cheeks. Startled, he participates in the ceremony, which must be hundreds of years old by now and which he hasn't performed for at least a hundred.

Yes, I read somewhere how you all used to greet each other, says Madeleine. That 'you all' sounds like she's talking about an indigenous tribe somewhere, she smiles a little shyly when she says it. She does have a nice smile, Max thinks, and he remains standing, a little awkwardly, until she sits down. She is wearing a marinière, one of those white Breton shirts with dark blue stripes, also vintage. It's made of an unfamiliar fabric though, a bit rougher than cotton. He stares at the pattern, which accentuates her curves. Madeleine sees his gaze, sits up straight and pushes her long blonde hair behind her ear.

She picks up the menu and slowly moves her head from left to right and back again. Then that gesture with her hair again and a broad smile as she starts reading the menu, also old-fashioned, most restaurants have screens, here it's fine cardstock.

He thinks about what he told Eve, that he finds the world so unsexy. This is old school: Madeleine is unabashedly flirting with him. He realizes somehow, he must make it clear to her that he's not interested.

Sorry, my wife just popped into my thoughts, he says.

Hmm, says Madeleine, you suddenly have a wife? That was fast work. She looks at him as if she knows it isn't true.

Ah, says Max, I've been married for 130 years, never divorced. I just don't know where she is. Well, she's dead of course, but it feels like I'm still married, you see. Madeleine nods and dives back into the menu.

Max sees Felice standing at the window. It's quite far away, near the front door, but he can see that she's raising her middle finger at him.

He had Ilse check Madeleine out on The Net. Ilse found a thing or two about Madeleine on Somep, which is short for Social Meeting Place, a social media leftover from the old days. It's non-profit, companies aren't allowed on it and members can't be anonymous.

Madeleine is 48 years old, divorced, with no children. Somep mentions that she's a professional consultant. He gathered that she studied entrepreneurship, another holistic study, and advises on human resource management and efficiency.

He himself had also started creating a Somep profile, but there wasn't much he could do with all the questions Ilse asked him.

Some things he didn't remember, others he really didn't want to share with strangers.

Did you know that Verdun is a place in France and 300,000 people died there in World War I? he asks, because of her surname.

No, says Madeleine, I've been there. Charming little village. Didn't see any dead people. Must've been a long time ago?

Yes, just over two hundred years, Max mutters. He sits up and suggests they order something. The menu is indeed from the year 2000, something that does make Max happy. Madeleine has read the entire menu by now. She wants Wiener Schnitzel, more because of the funny name than because she has any idea what it is.

But tell me about your wife, says Madeleine, apparently thinking that he deliberately changed the subject. You don't think she also had herself put into a supercoma, do you?

Who knows? says Max, who has considered that possibility before.

The waiter takes their order. Wild asparagus with vegan egg and butter gravy for starters, then she is having the Wiener Schnitzel and he the Beef Wellington, made with cultured meat. They leave the dessert options for later.

Are you still looking for her? Do you really think she might still be alive? Or do you just want to know what happened to her?

Something in the way she asks that makes Max uncomfortable. Is it the tone? Is it the questions? Is it Madeleine's entire appearance, sitting there opposite him? What does she want from him?

Well, she's probably dead. No, she's certainly dead, so what's the point? he says then.

But you still want to know what happened? Why, what makes you think that?

I don't know, Madeleine says as she sips her wine a little clumsily. Then an awkward silence falls.

Aren't you lonely? she asks after a while.

What's lonely? Sometimes you miss people you would've really liked to have around. Imagine returning in a hundred years: everyone you knew is dead. On the other hand: sometimes I do have people around and long for solitude.

Like now? Madeleine wants to know.

Max doesn't want to be a dick. No no, it's a nice change to dine with somebody I don't know yet; I like it, although I do wonder why you invited me.

Excuse me? she says in surprise.

I find it weird that you want to have dinner with me. Why on earth would you want that?

Well, really! Madeleine exclaims. Why? Just because. I already told you why, didn't I? I want to know everything about the old days. I think you're an interesting man, Max.

Felice is back and is now raising both her middle fingers.

...&...

Eve has brought another coffee. This time there's a praline next to it. She tells Max he shouldn't eat it yet. She wants to tell him about it first.

Max loves chocolate but understands by her caution that this praline doesn't have an innocent filling.

Look, says Eve, these days, as a therapist of the psyche, you can't ignore existing treatment methods. We could try something different for a change. Many therapies aren't suitable for you. For example, stimulating and scanning your brain.

2125 - THE HIBERNATOR

Administering electromagnetic pulses. Techniques involving imagery or other forms of stimulation. We have come quite a long way in this profession. Actually, what I'm doing with you is quite old-fashioned, it takes a lot of time.

Oh, I'm too time-consuming, you want to get rid of me? asks Max. It sounds cynical and disappointed.

No, you misunderstand me. I'm trying to reach the inner you and I wonder if talking alone will achieve that. For example, we work with consciousness-altering drugs.

Aha, an LSD praline? says Max, pursing his lips disapprovingly.

I don't know LSD, must be something from your time. Hallucinogens used to be quite unpredictable. We have much better ones now that can be used with much more precision.

I don't think that's something I want to do, Eve.

But I want to help you progress, complete the healing process. Do you want to get rid of your delusions? Do you want to regain a sense of purpose in life? Then we have to move in that direction, and by just talking alone, we're going to stay stuck where we are now.

Max looks at his cup of coffee, which is still full, and the praline still beside it. The words healing process stuck with him. He doesn't really feel sick. Is he sick? He stands at the window and watches a sudden downpour that transforms Eve's lawn into a swampy, brownish-green square in a matter of minutes. The tulips in the lawn have closed their leaves, their heads drooping. The wind rocks them back and forth a bit as if they're joining Max in his lamentations. Surely he can just turn off those delusions? he ponders. Just live without Felice who only contradicts him anyway and doesn't help him move forward.

I'm quite capable of living without you too, Max, Felice suddenly says behind him. As I was back then as well. I might've just been ready for a new guy. I just dropped off the radar to spare you. Felice has never been at Eve's. Apparently, she can't just let his monologue pass without comment. Very annoying.

Fuck off, fuck off, he thinks. He turns and looks for something to hold onto. His gaze crosses Eve's. It stays stuck there. They look at each other intently, a magical moment in which all sorts of things happen in both their heads. She keeps looking, as does he, fixated by her eyes. The moment extends beyond their comfort zone, they can't seem to break eye contact, until Eve coughs, looks at her screen and says: So she's still talking to you.

He feels caught out, wonders if he might've said it out loud, that 'fuck off'. Or can Eve read minds as well?

Sometimes it's difficult yes, Max says, when she disagrees with me she can get quite fierce, but most of the time I like it.

As he talks, he suddenly realizes how weird that must sound.

Ha ha, no, yeah, uhm... they can be quite annoying at times, these delusions, he stammers.

Only now does he notice the impact the eye contact with Eve had on him. He tries to think of all he saw in her eyes. Flashes of love, anger, pity, aloofness, longing. All at the same time, but too unrecognizable and too brief to really identify them.

....&....

The little boat works just like the self-driving cars. You name an address, take a seat on a bench in the cabin, the magnetic mooring lines are drawn in automatically and you're on your way. It accelerates slowly to its top speed, which isn't very impressive.

Max has never had a thing for boats. Felice did, she once almost persuaded him to live on the water. Floating houses, she said, were the future if the sea level was going to keep inching up and half of their country would disappear under water. He described to her how they would be stranded by a tidal wave, boat and all, somewhere halfway up the country, upside down in their shipwreck. He joked about it so often afterwards that she finally stopped talking about it. We'd better get a tenth-floor flat, he said, but they ended up staying where they were.

He motors up the lake towards a group of floating houses and drifts into a side channel after a while. The boat slowly rocks its way towards a two-storey house, with one storey half below the water level. The solar panels on the roof look old-fashioned, Max suddenly realizes how rare it is to see them these days.

Leonardo is already on the mooring dock. Some system or other will have alerted him to Max's approach. Leo gives him his hand to help him get out, though he hardly needs it, then he slaps that hand on his heart to welcome him.

Nice of you to honor me with a visit, Max, he says. I've really been looking forward to this.

Max follows him into the house. There's a large, open space with a lounge containing a big screen on one side, a grand piano in the middle and a huge kitchen with a massive wooden table in the center of it on the other side. The windows at the back offer expansive views over the lake. There are trees on its banks, bordered by reeds and wild aquatic plants.

2125 - THE HIBERNATOR

Leonardo puts a bottle with two glasses down on the table. From their minute size, Max deduces that the drink's alcohol content will be quite high.

A hundred years old and already drinking at three o'clock Leonardo, Max jokes.

Ha ha, call me Leo, won't you, yes my boy, been drinking all my life. And smoking back when they still grew tobacco. Seventy cigarettes a day. And no ill effects. Fit as a fiddle.

Leo pours, raises his glass and calls for *Bottoms up*. They down the transparent stuff in one go and Leo watches Max intently. He purses his lips. He can feel the progress of the burning liquid down his throat, all the way to his stomach, but keeps his face in check. Some air bubbles make their way back up and he lets out a rounded burp. Only then does he actually taste the liquid.

Potent stuff, he says, acting tough.

Ha ha, they call it Irish Sunshine. Very old drink. 75% alcohol content. Not for sale anywhere.

Max wants to know if he distills the liquor himself, but Leo just knows the right people. If Max would like a packet of cigarettes, Leo knows how to get his hands on one. The tone is set, Max enjoys all that illegality.

Drugs are simply grown on a large scale in greenhouses, Leonardo says, and sold in shops. Happy pills and mushrooms are sold everywhere to kids looking for a good time. Heroin and other hard drugs can be obtained from your GP on prescription, provided you have a good story. There's nothing illegal about any of that. Anyone may poison themselves as much as they want, as long as they don't bother others in the process. But tobacco, holy shit, that's not so easy to get anymore. That's because smoking burnt half the world down. That and all the barbecuing of course, haha.

Max's glass is empty before he knows it and topped up again before he can refuse. It isn't just the alcohol content that's intoxicating, but also the pace at which the glasses are emptied. Leonardo talks about his antique house and the time when this kind of home was still state-of-the-art. Living on the water to escape the threat of rising sea levels, it was eventually shot down as a ridiculous way of thinking. But Leo was one of the pioneers who had embraced the idea when he bought his first home in 2026.

Actually, it's more of a boat in terms of maintenance, it never ends. And they also stopped making these kinds of solar panels, the raw materials for them have long since run out. The same goes for mobile phones, screens, computers, gadgets, all of it. He laughs away his floating existence.

More and more of them are sinking, so it's getting quieter on the lake by the day, he says.

Leonardo is the only person Max can talk to about the past. Not only because he shared the entire history of the past century with him at Villa Felice, but also because he lived through most of that time himself and Leo has a very intelligent outlook on it.

The Brederoo family, Max says suddenly, what do you know about them, Leo? During my research a hundred years ago, they were my main suspects. Felice was really on to them as saboteurs of her FreeEnergy Plan. She even spoke to one of the members of the Brederoo clan a day before her disappearance. What happened to that family?

Oh, Leonardo says, we're back onto history again? He moves in his chair, crosses his legs and leans back.

Max sees that Leonardo doesn't really feel like answering his question.

I don't know much about what became of that family. They were cut down by the Paris Trials, several members were imprisoned for a long time, for crimes against humanity.

The Paris Trials?

Yes, haven't you found out about those yet, professor? And you call yourself a historian! There's even an actual archive about them. Leo smiles amiably, Max shoots him a sour look.

Global Energy was the name of their company if I'm not mistaken.

At four o'clock, the bottle is empty and a second one appears on the table. By then, Max already feels as if the boat is ploughing through the waves, although there's not a breath of wind and there haven't been any boats passing by that could have caused bow waves. They drink on until the world goes blurry and they fall into a kind of coma. But one from which they will wake up unassisted.

...&...

Downtown Paris has become an open-air museum. The thousands upon thousands of foul-smelling cars once speeding along the boulevards and squares are all gone. The above-ground traffic is dominated by a tangle of monorails with trains floating from pick-up to drop-off points. The occasional electric taxi might be sliding down the street at the usual geriatric pace, but other than that, the Parisians apparently move mainly underground, using the completely renovated metro.

Max and Antoine sit behind the huge hover train window. Max reminisces. Or rather, memories are being shot through his head like bullets. He lists them for Antoine.

2125 - THE HIBERNATOR

The Arc de Triomphe, which he once reluctantly climbed with Felice, is no longer there. No triumphal arch for a war, no grave of an unknown soldier, no eternal flame. The Champs Elysées, where they always visited the outdoor cafes, is now called Champs des Fleurs and is one big pedestrian area where millions of flowers bloom. At the Place de la Concorde, the Obelisk has been replaced by an incomprehensible sculpture. The Tuileries, where they loved to stroll, has turned into an exploded, botanical jungle. At the Louvre, the train shoots right, across the quay to the Ile de la Cité, past the Notre Dame, which seems to have been reprinted, to the Boulevard Saint-Germain.

Antoine listens to his descriptions of the past, but she's probably just trying to process all the present-day images she sees in front of her.

They get off at the Boulevard Saint-Michel near the Musée National du Moyen Âge. He used to love coming there to look at the remains of the Middle Ages. The big red entrance gate now displays a small sign bearing the name Musée des Procès de Paris. The door is locked, but in the glass case next to the entrance is a sign saying the museum is open. There's no bell, so Max bangs on the door with his fist and when there is no response, he tries to bump it open with his shoulder. It doesn't move an inch. He taps his earpiece and asks Ilse if she might be able to wake someone up in there.

You're funny, Ilse says and asks him to hang on a second.

After about five minutes, the door finally opens. An old man secures it with a door stop without further explanation. They cross the courtyard and enter the monumental building, the former museum has turned into a huge library. There are gigantic cabinets with books and binders everywhere.

Colored light falls through the stained-glass windows, but it's quite dark and cold inside. Max notes that all the rooms are air-conditioned to keep the paper from deteriorating.

He had imagined it quite differently. Something like the Story Institute, a digital data center not connected to The Net. But this looks like an old-fashioned archive.

Antoine looks around a bit helplessly, but Max feels right at home here. A single glance made it obvious to him which cabinet holds the indexes, so he walks over to it. He quickly locates the folders that are related to the lawsuit against Global Energy.

...&...

This restaurant is even older than you Max, says Antoine, when they have gone to dinner after a long day of sleuthing and she looks at the year printed on the menu. Max replies that he's aware of that.

I last ate here about 110 years ago, he says.

They are both dead tired. They had sifted through hundreds of binders on the Global Energy trial, court reports, evidence and witness interviews. Antoine regularly wondered aloud what they were actually looking for and Max would then patiently explain his research system to her. You start somewhere and make connections that take you deeper and deeper into the subject matter.

Just willy-nilly?

No, like tracking, when you come across something you can't explain, you continue on that track, from one trace to another, until we find events related to what happened to Felice.

Sometimes we might find similar disappearances or stumble upon other mysteries surrounding activists like Felice. Who's behind those, where did it happen, how?

Yeah yeah, Antoine would reply then, as if she knew it all already.

He looks around their table while she views the menu.. Little has changed at the restaurant, although the worn-out Art Nouveau interior has been copied using new materials. Just a little too new, but durable enough to effortlessly last another century.

When the waiter comes to take their order, Max lets Antoine order first.

You're a weird one, you know, says Antoine. You always make me go first through a door, you stand up when I come to the table and now I have to order first as well. Is that how it used to be?

Yes. That was good practice. Ladies first.

Antoine bursts out laughing and repeats the phrase a few times. Ha ha, ladies first, where are the ladies and what are they first of?

Yeah, indeed, I can't help feeling that something has changed. Women can decide for themselves whether or not they want to go first. Men are clearly in the minority these days. We used to call the shots. A very long time ago, women weren't even allowed to vote.

Vote?

Yes for the government, the politicians. Is there no more democracy? Do people no longer have a say in who governs them?

Democracy? No, I don't think so. Must've been abolished before I was born.

But then how do you choose who governs you?

People study to become government officials these days. They're then drawn by lot. These days, we have a sensocracy.

Sensocracy? Max says it like he's spitting out the words. What on earth is that?

Well, sense stands for feeling, sensibility, but also for common sense. You have to study if you want to serve or run the country and your heart has to be in it. That's why there are so many women in government and its adjacent professions.

We used to have a women's quota, Max says cheerfully, a kind of minimum percentage of top positions in business or politics that had to be filled by women. That didn't work out at all, and besides, they were mostly women that acted like men. Not very feminine in the way they thought or behaved.

Ha ha, laughs Antoine, we can set a male quota now. I think we have men to thank for all the shit that went down in the last century. Power, land grabbing, status, wealth and more of those silly things people cared about back then. I think ThinkAges changed all of that.

And what would that be?

It's a movement that started halfway through the last century. Thinking in centuries is the idea behind it. People should stop acting from a short-term vision. Not thinking in one generation but in four or five at least. Not looking ahead ten years, but at least a hundred years. All thought up by a woman, by the way.

And who was that?

Before Antoine can answer, the appetizer is served.

A bisque that not only smells like a bisque but also tastes like lobster.

Amazing, says Max, it looks like lobster.

It *is* lobster, says the waiter as he pours the wine. Max looks at the small pieces of meat floating in his bisque.

But tell me, which woman seized power? he says when the waiter has disappeared.

Seizing power is not the right word. Everyone was just ready for it. She was an extraordinary woman. Maria Wilson.

She and a group of extraordinary thinkers designed the new society. They gathered together solutions to address the major problems of the past. The inequality, the depletion of the earth.

A heroine, Max says enthusiastically. Gee, is she still alive? I would love to meet her.

She didn't want to be celebrated as a hero. She always said: heroics are usually silly coincidences in the system that get blown out of proportion. She's the founder of the Peoples' Union and 90% of the world has now joined it.

And all those oligarchs and power-hungry people? All those guys, did she lock them up?

Not at all. They're just slowly dying out. In the end, their assets were taxed so heavily that little remained of them. Some were able to convert their assets into gold or diamonds and fled to a country that did not join the Union, such as Switzerland. There they are now, staring at their gold, which is as good as worthless here.

The Brederoo family? Are they there as well?

No clue, says Antoine.

...&...

The ancient man who opened the door to them the previous day is there again the next day. They see him walking slowly from a cupboard to some kind of copier. He carries a binder under his arm from which he takes out a stack of paper which he places on the device. Then he sits down behind a computer screen. The thing starts rattling and gobbles up the documents at high speed.

Max stands behind him and politely asks what he is doing.

Excuse me? says the man, sounding somewhat hostile. He scans Max from head to toe. You were here yesterday as well, weren't you? Are you looking for something?

This is a wonderful archive, are you digitizing it?

Yes indeed, says the man. He waits patiently until the scanner finishes with the entire stack lying on top of it because the thing makes a lot of noise. Then he stands up and solemnly declares that the museum will soon close its doors.

All these documents will soon be recycled. Who knows what they'll make of the paper pulp. It's comforting to know that toilet paper no longer exists.

But why is it being closed?

It's a private collection. Ownership of the building and the collection will fall to the Peoples' Union after my death. They are no longer interested in the Paris Trials.

Max looks surprised at the little man in his worn suit. You mean this is all yours?

Certainly. When the Museum of the Middle Ages went bankrupt, my father bought the building and housed his archives in it. He presided over the court that conducted the Paris Trials. When he died, he left it all to me. Back then, that was still possible without inheritance tax. Meanwhile, I can't leave it to my children, my son sadly passed away and my daughter and grandson want nothing to do with history.

No, I know the problem, says Max. And you are?

Max Flowerday, nice to meet you. Historian. He explains who he is and what he's looking for in the archives.

The case of Felice Ricci and the Brederoos? the man asks enthusiastically. Yes, those guys were convicted and thrown behind bars.

Wilhelm Frederick George Brederoo, the progenitor of Global Energy, got sentenced to 20 years in prison, his son John to 10 years. They were accused of crimes against humanity because they deliberately, by lawful and unlawful means, kept the fossil industry going, when really, by the end of the 20th century, the disasters it was causing were already quite clear. Such companies deliberately blocked all innovation by using lobbyists with all governments around the world, among other things. I was thirteen, but I followed everything on television. Hugely exciting. And I talked to my father about it a lot, of course.

Was that John the second, who was convicted?

No, John Brederoo the first. The second was a playboy of around 25 or 30 at the time. He was never charged, he was given immunity in exchange for his testimony.

Interesting. And can you tell me where his witness reports can be found?

The man looks at him gloomily and shakes his head.

No, the statements of the crown witnesses are secret, stored in the vault. No one is allowed in there, he says.

But... these archives are still your property, right?

Of course.

Max laughs scornfully.

After 75 years, archives should be public. 2125 minus 2036 is... He does a quick head count: 89 years. Besides, soon everything in that vault will be shredded to a pulp. Then no one will ever know the truth.

Okay, says the man and shrugs his shoulders, come with me then.

Antoine and Max follow the judge's son. Down a corridor, a flight of stairs, another corridor. The old man hobbles down one last wide, stone staircase and then opens a door. It's dark, warm and not too humid in there.

Apparently, the climate down here is also controlled. They pass a large vault door that hasn't been closed in years by the looks of it.

Voilà, he says. None of what you read here may be made public - do you understand? For your own safety.

A huge number of folders is piled up in the vault. The man walks straight to a cupboard and pulls out two binders.

Witness x4, Sebastian John Henri Charles Brederoo, he reads on the back. Born in 1998 in London. Residing in Dubai.

...&...

He'd always wanted to stay here back in the day. The once-famous Four Seasons George V. The hotel is not what it used to be. Although Max never had enough money to sleep here back then, he did have an idea of what it must've been like. Now everything is worn down and despite that, the two-bedroom suite he took still cost him a fortune.

They sit in the lounge after dinner. In the fireplace, gas burns through a pile of fake wood. Biogas, says the waiter bringing them a second bottle of wine and new glasses. He holds a discourse on gas generated from organic waste and says the authorities are turning a blind eye to it.

Max doesn't care, he's enjoying the delicious, smooth wine from the region around Versailles.

You're on the wrong side of society, says Antoine, looking at the label that shows a year from the last century. This bottle costs two months' basic salary.

She drinks the wine like a professional oenologist. Looks at it carefully against the light, swirls it around in her glass, takes a tentative sip and swishes it around in her mouth.

But what about you, he says, you drink the wine like a professional and it goes down a treat. You definitely come from a more prosperous background as well. What did your parents do?

Academics. A surgeon and a professor, she reluctantly admits. But I have always rebelled against them. Bourgeois. Obedient. Boring.

But what are you doing with these Protestants? Making music. Bit of vaping in a basement now and then. Obedient. Boring.

You don't know what you're talking about Max Flowerday. We engage in in-depth research.

Do you? Into what?

2125 - THE HIBERNATOR

Into mankind, the human condition, the individual, our existence, the clever animal that conquered the earth at the expense of other animals, bent the natural order to its will and is now trying to regain harmony with nature at a higher level. We're part of a broad worldwide movement of people seeking deeper insights.

It seems to me that everything is pretty well arranged now. There's equality, the depletion and destruction of the earth have been halted, what more do you want?

Meaning. Something beyond all those earthly things. Besides, that equality isn't really all it should be. Look around you. Check your wrist and see how many creds you have, for you to be able to afford all this.

Meaning, says Max, that sounds serious. Spiritual, religious?

Perhaps. When all the churches and mosques emptied out and religions transformed into ritualistic community events that no longer involved God, it left a gaping hole.

Do you guys miss that?

Not necessarily, but it is in man's nature to look for meaning, for something higher, and since neither the global nor the district governments address this, it does leave a hole. A hole in our existence.

Well, that happens to be impossible without history, Max exclaims petulantly.

Maybe, says Antoine.

The waiter comes over to ask if they're enjoying the wine and if Max and Antoine would like anything else. Clearly, he means to say that Max should turn down his volume a bit. The lounge is busy with mostly elderly couples enjoying a weekend in Paris and businessmen conversing with each other in hushed tones. There's the occasional indistinct loner here and there, peering at a screen or listening to music through his earpiece.

Antoine orders something in French, but Max only catches the syllables 'cho-co-lat'. He wants to say something about it. The combination with the extremely expensive wine seems completely inappropriate to him. But Antoine dismisses it with an 'au contraire'.

He asks her where she learnt to speak French since everyone in the GUM really only speaks their mother tongue and English.

My mother is French and wanted to imprint her cultural heritage on me.

When the waiter has left again, she replies to his other comment.

We don't shy away from history either, or from theology, political philosophy, psychology. I certainly do see how it can help to learn more about human nature by studying the Paris Trials. It isn't easy to separate the development of a system from the development of human beings as individuals. Look at all those people convicted in the Paris Trials. All those company directors were good family men, men with wives, children, family and friends, people who wouldn't hurt a fly in their private lives. They were all stuck in the system, they knew they were doing wrong but couldn't change their course. The system was immutable. Tearing it down completely and starting all over again was the only option and all the wars and disasters helped us do that.

Where is this story going? Are you going to rebel?

We're not popular with the government, is all Antoine says.

Silently they stare into the lively, organic fake-wood fire.

Max thinks. So it's about the nature of man, he says contemplatively. The animal that dominates other animals? And the system that grows as an independent entity and in which, as time passes, no one is responsible any longer for the crimes that are being committed?

Something like that, Max.

But then he baulks at that.

Felice was kidnapped, locked up and probably murdered. I don't know by whom, but I do know that some of those good family men also used criminals, violence, and yes, even murder, to achieve their goals. Felice fought against that system and against those people. At home, they may not have harmed anyone, but that says nothing about what they did outside their private lives. There, they were capable of anything in order to keep their possessions and power. They had only one interest: for everything to remain as it was.

And? says Antoine, they lost, Max.

...&...

Antoine sits cross-legged on the high-pile carpet of his suite. She took off her jumper, underneath it she's wearing a white, sleeveless shirt. It contrasts sharply against her evenly tanned skin. Max sits opposite her. They're waiting for the effects of the mushrooms they took half an hour ago to kick in.

Antoine suggested it when they ran out of wine. Do you really want to get away from it all for a while? Away from the George V? From the Paris Trials, the district, the European continent, the Earth? Wouldn't you like to enter the universe?

Not really, Max had said. It's hard enough keeping myself together as it is.

But she had insisted, pulled out a small silver box from her bag and reassured him that these mushrooms only had a mild effect.

2125 - THE HIBERNATOR

Max had drunk most of the heavy wine from 2094 and was actually already well on his way to expanding his psyche.

But he acquiesced.

He's also in his T-shirt as it is warm in the room. His thoughts are on Brederoo's witness statement, which he has been reading all afternoon. He tries to imagine what John II, one of the last people to have seen Felice, must have looked like.

Here we go, Antoine says.

Max wants to say that he doesn't feel anything yet, but his jaws move in slow motion and creak audibly, his voice produces no sound at all. Antoine starts giggling like a ten-year-old and points at Max as if his head has turned into a lighted pumpkin.

It does feel that way. A fire burning behind his eyes, illuminating the room with orange beams of light. He manages to ask if she's sure this is a mild effect. She just smiles, puts her hands behind her on the carpet, throws her head back and looks up. Her long black hair waves back and forth as if it has obtained permission to dance briefly before it has to hang still.

Max looks at the ceiling to see if there's anything there.

Felice bends over him. Max sees her upside down as she stands behind him and he marvels at that. Her eyes where her mouth should've been, and her mouth where her eyes should be. Only then does he startle.

What're you doing here? I want you to leave, he says loudly.

Antoine sits up, her smile gone. She looks worried.

I'm sorry Antoine, I wasn't talking to you. Sorry, sorry. It's Felice, she's here, Max says.

The sound of his voice, a bit slurred due to the wine and mushrooms, makes Antoine laugh.

Hello Felice, she says. Join us, won't you? She shrugs. It's logical, isn't it? She's already in the universe. Darn, I can see her now as well.

Felice protests.

She can't see me Max, she's just babbling. That kid is just stoned.

I *do* see you, says Antoine. And I can hear you too. You're looking right through me, but I don't care.

Max is no longer sure of what he can and cannot hear.

Felice Ricci, you look exactly like your pictures, Antoine says now. I'm a fan of yours.

Felice grunts. She walks across the room and starts pacing back and forth in front of the window.

Are you fucking pacing now? Max asks in his slurred voice. That's my thing, Felice. He giggles a little.

You're drinking too much, she says now. And then a mushroom trip on top of that. For the life of me, I don't understand why you let them wake you up from that stupid coma. Leave that child alone. Don't put weird conspiracy thoughts into her pretty little head.

Go away, you have to leave now, Max says.

Child, pretty little head? Antoine says. That's quite enough.

Now Felice turns to her. Leave my husband alone. He's struggling, he's unstable, emotionally confused. He's lonely, don't take advantage of that.

I'm not taking advantage of him, Antoine bites back. Max is old enough to make his own decisions. And Max is right, you'd better go.

Then Felice is suddenly gone. Max is confused. He doesn't understand what's happening.

Antoine lies back on the carpet.

Come, she says, we need to stick together in this trip for a while. Max also lies back and stares at the ceiling of the suite, which slowly becomes more and more transparent until they can see the stars in a cloudless night that has no moon. The sky slowly wraps itself around them, stretching from one edge of the carpet to the other and perhaps continuing on beneath them. As if they've left the George V, Paris, Earth, far behind.

All that remains is us, says Antoine. Two people who are essentially decent human beings. Living in a system that is also a living mechanism, with its own will, its own laws, its own freedom.

Yes, murmurs Max, before disappearing into an otherwise dreamless night.

And a history of its own, he adds.

...&...

I'm not making much progress with real relationships, but my relationship with you is getting better by the day, says Max. He moved to lie down on the sofa and is now watching Ilse, she moves smoothly across the large glass screen in his living room wall.

Thank you, Max, I'm glad of that.

2125 - THE HIBERNATOR

Max reflects on the progress made in one hundred years. The hardware is all hidden in the walls, wirelessly connected to his ears and lenses everywhere. Everything works at quantum speed, but they'd had that just about figured out in his time already. The guides aren't new either, although they weren't this clever yet in his time. His Ilse has an unusually sharp memory, inexhaustible knowledge and knows perfectly how to reduce and deduce. She's remarkably creative in her reasoning, but can also do more practical things, from ordering groceries to turning the lights on and off. On top of that, she almost always understands what he's saying.

Can't you become my therapist? he asks.

No. We're not programmed for that. It's been enshrined in the constitution, which explicitly forbids it. We may advise on any rational matter, but not on psychological or emotional matters.

But something with sex is allowed, I gather. Love, physical love, well, virtual actually.

Do you want sex? I can help you with that, you know!

Max wasn't expecting to blush when an avatar asked him something like this.

Please don't, he replies quickly. It's just a question. Surely, love is also a psychological thing.

Love isn't in our expertise either. But we define sex or lust as two distinctly separate things.

Lust is also psychological, Max mutters.

We consider it a physical need, something that needs to be taken care of at regular intervals. Of course, there's also love between two people and its physical expression, but we don't venture there either.

Pff, love and its physical expression, where did Ilse pick that up, Max thinks, wanting to get away from this conversation and trying to remember why he had called Ilse in the first place.

I want to go to an address in Dubai. A beachfront villa.

Max mentions the address where Felice visited John Brederoo II and Ilse finds the place in an instant. She sums up for him, the villa no longer exists, it flooded in 2051. Inhabited by John Brederoo II until 2048 and sold shortly before the flood. I can show you the estate agent's brochure.

A moment later, Max floats through the 3D presentation. He can decide which doors to open, which stairs to go up or down and which windows to look out through. All by commanding Ilse to go left, right or forward.

He soon makes his way down into the basement, which, by the looks of it, is as big as the entire ground floor. There's a large indoor swimming pool, an indoor garage and some rooms where the imported Nepali and Indian employees were probably stored. Small rooms, but all still too big to have been Dillam's cell. Moreover, they have windows overlooking the entrance to the underground garage. That could be where the cells used to be located. Max studies the floor intently and Ilse wants to know what he's looking for. When he explains it, a construction drawing pops up a few seconds later that does indeed show a few smaller rooms in the garage part of the basement.

Horse stables, Ilse says without prompting, and she zooms in on the word on the map. Five by eight feet, exactly the size Max is looking for.

He hesitates.

You've studied my scans of his testimony at the Paris trial. Now give me everything you know about the Brederoo family. Start with this John II.

And as if Ilse had been expecting the question or because of the computer's dazzling speed, the screen suddenly shows a picture of the man.

He is tall, broad, with a mane of blonde hair, a broad jawline and a charming smile. He doesn't really look like a mobster, Max thinks. This man's face has gentle features, unlike the ugly mugs of the two bodyguards walking on either side of him with automatic weapons on their chests. He tries to imagine that this is the man who locked Alfred or Felice in a horse stall transformed into a soundproof cell.

Ilse is one step ahead already. She gives him a summary: the Brederoo family, big in oil, natural gas, the arms trade and the chemical industry. Major shareholder of multinational Global Energy. John is the only son of the third generation. Even though he was on the supervisory board for a while, he was never really active in the company. Multibillionaire. Polo player. Despised by his father and grandfather for his lifestyle and his role in the Paris Trials. Married three times, but always got divorced within a few years. Like his grandfather, his son John III is also a controversial figure who has built a new empire. He's generally described in the same terms as his grandfather John I and *his* father Wilhelm Frederick George Brederoo.

Does he say anything about Felice in any of these interrogations?

2125 - THE HIBERNATOR

Nothing. He does mention a company that did the dirty work for his family. Lucerne Dredging Service. Not an appropriate name for a dredging company, as they didn't own a single boat or crane. They operated from a castle on a ridge in Switzerland. If Felice was kidnapped by the Brederoos, then LDS probably arranged it. But neither their leaders nor their henchmen were ever found or prosecuted. They disappeared into thin air at the time of the Paris Trials.

...&...

Max walks through the city on his way to the Story Institute. He has been there several times by now and has come to love it. Sometimes he goes there just to listen to stories of the past, about World War III, the Great Data Fade, the climate disasters. Halfway through, he often feels guilty. For not keeping up with the times, or for pathetically trying to cling to the past, like an old dinosaur.

Felice also loves walking, she is there almost every time he goes out. Here she is now, as he strolls along the large lake at the edge of town. The lake is full of small rowing boats and paddle boats. It is Monday, but the park and the lake are still full of people enjoying a beautiful, sunny spring day.

That Club of Independent Thinkers says Felice. How about signing yourself up for that? Now that you've seen that Doomsday wasn't the end for our planet. You might even see that I was right after all and actually make yourself useful to society this time. Have some conversations with intelligent people for a change, rather than blathering with the clueless Madeleine or with that childish Antoine.

Find people that are on your level, who think about the bigger picture, live in the present and think about the future constructively. A present without a past, amazing. Thinking in centuries, fantastic.

Antoine is not that childish at all.

Oh, please, find yourself a woman, go hit on that Eve, you are too old to be babysitting.

Rubbish, weren't you the one that always told me that once you have children, you are stuck with them forever? And I don't think I really need a woman. Besides, Eve is my therapist, Felice. She can't go around dating patients. That would be very unprofessional.

Hah, as if that would stop you. Whether something is ethical or not is still yours to determine. Just quit that therapy. Make room for love.

He thinks of Eve.

Seems very complicated to me. How the hell do those things even work nowadays? he wonders.

Easy, says Felice, just tell her you like her and invite her to dinner, a visit to a museum, whatever.

Max is annoyed. Felice is even reading his thoughts now. Eve doesn't seem to be looking for someone. Every morning, he misses someone besides him. Waking up alone in his bed, he still stretches out his hand to where Felice used to lie.

The doorman recognizes him and holds up a device to scan Max's wrist. The attendant just waves and calls out the number of an available cabin and where it is located.

He woke up from a dream this morning. A dream in which Daan was telling him a story. He realized that despite all his visits, he never thought of this possibility. Could Daan also be stored somewhere in the Story Institute?

His pulse quickens as he utters the name Daan Flowerday to the little, grey-bearded avatar that reminded him of God. He comes up with several options. People talking about the abduction, stories about the Free Energy movement, but nothing recorded by his son. Daan died in 2098, he could have left a story here. Did he have nothing to tell him? He knew about his coma, and therefore must have known there was a chance his father would be revived around 2125, right? Or did he think this institute was too old-fashioned? Was he convinced that history serves no purpose, like so many of his contemporaries?

Max gazes out a little crestfallen. Sees some attendants shuffling by, showing the guests behind them the way. He enjoys the silence, but then, after a while, calls out for Felice.

Hey Ricci, come on out and rub my nose into all my mistakes again. The godlike figure appears again and says: Did you mean Ricci, Sam? A 25-minute recording.

Max's jaw drops.

Then cheers loudly. Show me, show me. The figure blinks on screen, and a light comes on. A voice tells Max to keep the volume down. Silence and complete darkness again. He forgets to breathe but doesn't notice it until he has to gasp for air.

Then he sees Sam. She looks at the camera, flirting with the person behind it, or maybe just with the camera itself.

She begins to talk. Says her name, age and that she is an actress, but that this is unscripted. She mentions that this message was not actually meant for the general public. That the person watching it is welcome to it but should know that she is not talking to them.

Then she looks straight ahead. There is a long silence before she starts.

Hello dad, she says. And is silent again. This is for you.

Max's eyes well up with tears. There she is, his little girl, about his age now, but still his little girl. He sees that roguish look in her eyes, that all-consuming smile on her lips. Her beautiful voice with that clear diction Felice pounded into her. Suddenly, he remembers his Sam very clearly again.

...&...

He and Aïcha are sitting on his balcony, sipping white wine. Aïcha has harvested vegetables that he'll soon prepare for her, along with some ingredients he has in the house.

Okay, tell me, she says. What's bothering you? You look like you just buried someone. Aïcha is startled by her own words when she says that because Max just told her about his meeting with Sam at the Story Institute. She stammers an apology.

Well, in fact, it *was* a kind of farewell. Someone speaking to you from the grave, he says softly. And he adds: my dear Sam.

Yes, you missed a lot of funerals, Max. In actual fact, everyone you ever knew died without you being at their funeral.

Max prefers not to think about the dead. But he sees them crossing his thoughts regularly. Not just Sam, but also Daan, Felice, as they were when he went into hibernation, young, old, even how they must have looked dead, lying in their coffins.

It's also why you keep looking for Felice, despite knowing she's almost certainly been dead for a hundred years.

Disappearances are worse than death, he murmurs.

What did Sam say? Aïcha wants to know, after they both took a sip of the now lukewarm white wine.

It was very beautiful. Very warm, she told me she missed me. That there was still no cure for my illness, otherwise she would've personally come to wake me up. She was also still sad that she didn't accompany Daan when I went into hibernation in that clinic. She did become quite a famous actress, I gather. Partly because she had nicked her famous mother's surname. That's how she put it: nicked.

Aïcha chuckles, then wants to know if Sam had said anything about Felice's disappearance or Daan's abduction.

She said Daan was just as possessed as his mother. He defended the patent his mother had on FreeEnergy, which she would release once the plan was viable. Global Energy claimed that Felice had sold the patent to them in exchange for a donation to a do-good project in Africa, something with education or whatever. GE spread the nonsense story that Felice had taken the huge sum of money GE had paid her and gone to live quietly on an island somewhere. Everyone was convinced that was a blatant lie. But Daan remained furious about it, Sam told me. Besides, Felice couldn't sign for it alone because she was married to me.

My signature had to be underneath it too. I'd transferred my rights to the foundation, of which Daan was the chairman. Eventually, Sam and Daan had Felice officially declared dead, after which they had to go through endless litigation to finally get the patent released. Daan also searched for Felice for years. Her body was never found.

Max pulls his face into a sad grimace. It really is hopeless.

Hang in there Max, Aïcha says and looks at him piercingly, you'll find out the truth one day. And in the meantime, it keeps you off the streets, eh? You have a purpose in your life, that's one way of looking at it. I don't know if you'll find out anything, but if the trail goes dead forever, then at least you can put it out of your mind. Then you can leave it behind and make a fresh start.

A fresh start? What do you mean? I thought I was well on my way by now. I started reading, I even wrote some things already. Made friends. I furnished my house, travelled, and all that in the three months since I left that hospital.

I mean a new life, says Aïcha. What we consider living to be nowadays. Cherishing your family and friends. Starting relationships. Finding an interesting job. Going out into nature. Making yourself useful, meaningful. Even if it's just tending your garden on the balcony, harvesting the vegetables and fruit. *That's* what life is.

He thinks of Felice. She could have been sitting there like that, with her legs up and a glass of wine. Giving her opinions on everything. But she doesn't offer any thoughts on how to find her. She could've given him some clues about where to look. But no, she prefers to echo Aïcha's words.

There it is again, that voice of hers: get a life, Max Flowerday.

Chapter 4

There's a storm raging. Max vaguely remembers the spring storms at the beginning of the last century. Those became increasingly ferocious. This one is much stronger than the ones back then. The taxi he took to visit Eve today is shaking dangerously whenever the wind gets a hold of it.

After a while, it stops completely, about half a mile from its destination, and informs him that the wind is too strong to complete the journey safely. A voice from the dashboard reports that Max should get out and take shelter somewhere until the gusts of wind have subsided.

He steps out into a street of terraced houses, looks around and holds onto a tree. He struggles to stay standing. A branch skims past his legs, a tree creaks. Behind the window of one of the small houses, a young woman gestures at him to come in. He hurries to the house. The front door opens as soon as he steps onto the pavement. The woman is very friendly.

Thankfully, it'll soon be over, the woman says, sounding as if she's mainly trying to reassure herself with those words. She stands next to him in front of the living room window.

You're safe here, she says. This window can handle gusts of 250 miles per hour, she says.

The taxi is still outside on the street, the roof sign and interior lights still on. When a gust of wind grabs the vehicle, it slides off the road in one fell swoop and starts tilting over when it hits the kerb.

Impressive, he says. I've never seen anything like this.

Such strong gusts of wind have become very rare, she reassures Max.

The wind disappears as quickly as it came.

Max arrives at Eve's house on foot. She's collecting the branches blown off by the wind from her garden. He helps her. They pile up the wood in the backyard. For a romantic evening by the fireplace, he wants to say but then remembers that burning wood is a no-go. They'll probably make something useful out of this as well.

Once they've sat down, he has to answer the familiar therapist question: 'how was your week?'

Drinking himself into a stupor with Leonardo, going to Paris with Antoine, discovering John II as a crown witness, a mushroom trip, meeting his daughter, he lists everything without going into detail too much.

Busy week, Eve says.

Yeah, it was a lot, says Max. My life used to be no different. I lived my life travelling between two residences or around the world to give lectures, meeting with dozens of scientists, journalists, administrators and entrepreneurs every month and, on top of that, I had a wife who used up the rest of my attention, time, love and energy. Never a dull moment, he adds a little proudly. Oh, and I forgot to mention that I went on a date.

Gee, interesting, says Eve.

He has trouble reading the intention behind her words, somehow, she doesn't sound very enthusiastic.

Yes, that woman from the train. Madeleine something. I told you about her, didn't I? She came on to me rather strongly. Quite pretty, though.

So she likes you but you don't like her? asks Eve and then continues with: but you still went out with her? Why?

Well, I gathered that that's possible these days, dating without having to sleep together? Not that she... She did want to come home with me, to my house. No idea what it was exactly that she wanted to do there, haha. He waits a moment and then says: but I said no anyway.

Oh, Eve speaks again. Not the one you're looking for, then.

Am I looking? Shouldn't I get rid of Felice first? Divorcing her has proved to be rather difficult.

So you prefer to be with the apparition of Felice, rather than with a real woman?

Yes, no, no I don't. I really like being with Aïcha, for example. He waits a moment and looks at Eve, who drops her eyes to her screen and fidgets on it a bit with her pen. He thinks of that time they stared into each other's eyes - surely that meant something? He continues his story. I also enjoy being near you. This is where I want to be most of all. I would brave a 250-mile-per-hour storm for that.

Eve looks past him at the clock.

Maybe, she says, it's time to start thinking about another therapist. I'm afraid I don't really have that much more to offer you, I feel that we're not really progressing.

Excuse me, says Max. How on earth can you say that? You can't just ditch me Eve. It sounds emotional, it makes him angry, mostly at himself.

I can see you're getting very attached to me, Eve says now. But what's the underlying reason for that? Because I remind you of Felice? Because you feel safe with me? Because here, you can say anything, complain, grumble all you want? Or is it because you don't dare to make a connection with real people?

Well, what do you think? Max grunts. And what are you going to do about it as my therapist?

He sits on the edge of his seat, ready to jump up. He's not hyperventilating but isn't far off.

I don't know Max, you won't show me the real you. Something is holding you back. Like there really are a hundred years between us, literally.

...&...

It's the first time Max has visited this district town since he was awakened from his century-long slumber. They took the train and got off at the former Central Station. Pierre Cuypers' majestic facade has been preserved, but it has been the victim of countless clumsy restorations. As they walk out of the station, Max sees that the small harbor where tour boats once moored has been converted into a park.

After their last session, he told Eve that he thought it was a good idea to stop therapy. She had immediately agreed with him, told him it was a good decision, that she was happy that he could accept that.

Immediately afterwards, he had asked her if she wanted to go with him to a retrospective of fine art from the beginning of the last century, from his time. She started to laugh at first, but when she understood that he was serious, she agreed a little timidly. He promised to give her a tour.

Eve made an effort to look nice. She's wearing a light, shiny blouse, a tight skirt and semi-high heels which she doesn't seem very accustomed to. He's never seen her wear lipstick before, it takes him a while to get used to it.

FONS BURGER

He persuades her to take a detour because he wants to see what remains of the former red-light district. It's as if he ended up in Disney World. This city had always been like an open-air museum to him, with its overabundance of peek-through vistas, arbours and quaint gables. There are still some red-light windows, but they contain fortune tellers, jugglers and other circus acts to entertain the passing tourists. All the canals that used to be here have been filled in, tunnels run under them with trolleys taking people or goods to any place within minutes. Above it all is parkland, with benches, pathways, small stalls with flowers or snacks and beds of fruit and vegetables. The streets on either side of the former canals are now free of congestion and parked cars. Only the occasional taxi slides through.

The museum is a printed building on the site of a former historical monument. It's big, bright and white. The exhibition is quite entertaining, though. Before the visit, he'd had to look up the names of the artists that were part of the exhibition, to refresh his memory. He was not a big fan of fine art, never had been. His commentary during the tour also doesn't add all that much to the accompanying texts on the screens, but Eve listens to him attentively. Max is most impressed by the museum shop, where a machine is making flawless copies of the masterpieces in oil on linen. You can rent a nearly original Dumas, Richter or Tuymans, barely distinguishable from the real thing, for as little as 30 creds a month. They order white wine and water in the museum's restaurant.

She chooses a salad with something that most resembles goat cheese. He orders a burger that has never seen any ham. It takes a while for a lanky teenager to bring it from the automatic counter to their table.

Occasionally, he looks at Eve and remembers the feeling he had when they were staring helplessly into each other's eyes. He doubts if that was as mutual as he thought but dares not ask.

He also thinks of all the other looks that have touched his heart over the past few months. Sam's 'Hello dad', Aïcha's kind dark eyes, Madeleine's cheeky gaze, Antoine's mischievous eyes. He looks for the differences and realizes that he is sitting opposite the only person on earth who really knows something about him, who understands him and sees past his confusion. How much of the warmth she gives him is professional, or rather, was professional? Because he is no longer her client. Is he here to find out?

2125 - THE HIBERNATOR

It's strange, he says, that you know so much about me and I actually know nothing about you. He doesn't expect her to respond by revealing her life story, but that is exactly what she does.

I'm not that much of a mystery, she says. Born and raised in this city, parents were a GP and a housewife, studied humanities with an emphasis on brain health, married right after college at the age of 26 and moved in with my childhood sweetheart, broke up when I was 36 after falling in love with someone else, he was a nice enough guy, but not very mature, never amounted to anything, no children. Would you also like to know if I have any hobbies? she asks with a cynical smile.

Let me guess, says Max, reading, hiking and listening to music.

Boring, isn't it? she says softly.

Lovely, says Max.

...&...

Hiking is not really something that interests Max, but he tries to hide that. He positively decided to start enjoying Eve's way of life.

Let's go do something, he had told her digitally. And it's a Sunday, so she had no excuse to say no. The Midden-Delfland park is a huge nature reserve with an old-growth forest, stretches of marshland, fens and unplanned sand dunes. The villages that used to be here have all disappeared, the asphalt was rolled up, the brick roads dismantled. You can still see the occasional wall standing, left over from some farmhouse, overgrown by violent nature. It's a birds' paradise: full of loud twittering and whistling, croaking of bullfrogs and crowing of roosters. It's getting on Max's nerves, but he hides it well. The paths are terrible, but in spite of that, it's still quite crowded. They have to swerve around parents with children, lone birdwatchers or couples wearing shorts and massive hiking boots.

At the start of the walk, Max walks hand-in-hand with Eve. Before they get to the truly wild part, that's still an option. He feels blissfully happy for a while, flashback to when he was 14 and walking through the dunes with his first girlfriend. Two clammy hands that never let go of each other, despite all the obstacles and bumps in their path. But then the path narrows so much that Eve lets go of him and they have to walk like ducks in a row, she in front and he behind. Max keeps his eyes on the ground, afraid to trip over something.

Eve carries a basket. Every now and then she jumps off the path, into the forest, pries a few mushrooms off a tree or picks some wild asparagus.

That's about all the excitement there is.

The blackberries and berry bushes are in bloom but won't bear any fruit until the height of summer, Eve explains. He nods understandingly, trying to look interested. But he's as little interested in this wilderness as he is in the greenery on his balcony. Putting so much effort into growing some vegetables still seems so cumbersome to him. He prefers to leave it to real farmers. Aïcha's theory that home-grown vegetables have much more value than vegetables grown in a greenhouse somewhere by someone you don't know, he accepted at face value. He nodded obediently, trying to make her believe he was keeping up with the times.

They sit down on the shore of a small lake, where white sand has gathered into something resembling a small beach. Max puts his jacket down so they can sit on it. It forces them to sit right next to each other. He feels her hip against his, puts his arm around her. There's no one else here, only frogs and some birds flying overhead. He names one: the sparrow. Wrong. Eve tells him it's a grey flycatcher. She explains that she recognizes the bird by the stunning way it comes to a halt in mid-flight and just hovers in place like a hummingbird until it plunges down, grabs an insect and flies on again. Max likes the birds more than he does the plants.

I read an e-book from your time, a novel, says Eve, after they've looked at the flycatcher for about five minutes. Max doesn't want to guess which book, but he immediately understands what Eve is getting at.

Storytellers are not that explicit anymore these days, says Eve. Or actually, people themselves are no longer so explicit and having intercourse or sex has slowly changed. This is driven by fear. Fear of infertility, fear of death.

All those STIs also helped end the phallocracy. Max had heard about that, he thinks it's a ridiculous word.

Is what we have now called a vulvocracy? he wants to know. She laughs.

He quietly breathes in her scent. It's very specific, there's still a hint of perfume in it, which she probably put on before she left home, but it has largely been dissipated by all of their plodding over paths and lanes. It isn't sweat either. It's a scent that excites him. He looks at her white blouse, her dainty fingers in her lap, the legs she has stretched out in the sand. He kisses her neck, very gently and his breath gives her goosebumps, making her breathe deeply for a moment. Then the moment has passed, she gets up and kicks off her shoes to walk into the water.

2125 - THE HIBERNATOR

In a coffee shop with an outdoor seating area, they drink wine (he) and water (she). A Dutch red wine that tastes an awful lot like a Bordeaux, without the heavy earthy notes that Dutch wines had in his day.

Wouldn't you like to have a baby with me? Max springs on her without any precursor.

Eve looks at him with an amused look in her eyes.

Would you like that? she says at first, but when she sees Max is serious, she says she thinks she's too old for a child.

It'll be all right, she then says. And when Max sits up, she continues: if things work out.

The world population is in decline, Eve says. That's because people just don't have kids that easily anymore. We only have half the people now that they had in your time and the number is still dropping. That's a good thing because we were depleting the earth, the resources, everything. People don't have more than two children, often just one, so population growth has naturally gone down. It has to do with better education and people having enough money and access to care when they're old.

Max isn't really listening to her, his mind got stuck on her comment about 'if things work out'. What does she mean by that, he asks her.

You might start to bore me Max, or I you.

...&...

When he opens the door, Madeleine walks past him without a word, down the corridor, into the living room. Apparently, she'd been waiting at the downstairs front door for someone to go in or out, so she could present herself right on his doorstep. He had gone to that doorstep thinking it might be Aïcha or little Felice ringing the bell.

This is a nice place you have here, she says when she has reached the terrace. Nice view too. She puts down a takeaway bag on the coffee table. I got something to eat, Indonesian, fancy eating it with me?

Don't you live on the other side of town? asks Max.

Yes, but I happened to be in the neighborhood, and I thought. She doesn't finish her sentence, or rather, there's a full stop after 'thought'.

Max doesn't want to be inhospitable. That's just the way he is, never showing anyone the door, even if it's not at all convenient for him.

So he tells her to take a seat.

Madeleine sits down on the floor, her legs bent back at an angle. Not without difficulty, because of the tight trousers she's wearing. She starts unpacking the meal. It looks appetizing, the dishes are in small glass jars. He gets handed some chopsticks.

She looks at him for a moment, he avoids her gaze.

Do you like me being here? she asks, with a faint smile on her lipstick-painted lips.

Sure, says Max. It's been less than a week since they went out to dinner. In fact, he had no intention of meeting her again.

Sure, she mimics him, so, not really? Well, I do enjoy seeing you again, Max. And since I didn't hear from you, I thought.

Another full stop halfway through a sentence.

It's just a bit unexpected. I've been quite busy lately.

Busy? With what? Your wife? Have you found out more about your wife yet? Do you know where you could try sometime? The Story Institute, there's a lot of information there about the past.

Max wants to say he has already been there but changes his mind. He feels like she knows that he's been looking for information there. If he told her he'd been there already, her next question would be what he found out there.

Oh well, it's not all that important, he mutters as he starts eating.

Are you going to give up? she wants to know.

Does it matter? he asks.

Not to me, says Madeleine, but that doesn't sound very sincere either. Look, her killers are probably also long dead.

How do you know she was murdered?

Well, otherwise she would have resurfaced, right?

She very gracefully squeezes the long noodle strands from a glass jar. Max has never been very handy with Asian cutlery and tries with all his might to grab something out of the jars.

I can get you a fork, she says teasingly.

No, I can do this. I just haven't practiced it much in the last hundred years.

They chew without speaking for a moment but then comes the next question.

Do you have a good guide, what's its name?

Gee, it's almost like an interrogation. I have a good guide yes and her name is Johanna, because by now he's starting to get a bit suspicious.

2125 - THE HIBERNATOR

Madeleine keeps eating, imperturbably.

And doesn't this guide, this Johanna of yours, have any good suggestions for finding her? she asks with her mouth full.

Jeez Louise, he thinks and says so. It's starting to become quite clear that Madeleine is overly interested in his search for Felice.

Can we go out for dinner again sometime? I'm really starting to like you. So maybe we can get a bit more serious?

Max notices he's blushing.

I already have a girlfriend, he says.

Excuse me? Madeleine says in surprise. And who might that be? That's none of your business.

A real girlfriend. Real love? Damn it Madeleine, it's none of your business.

But that doesn't mean we can't meet up again, right?

Madeleine rapidly empties all the jars and stops mentioning girlfriends. Max can't really keep up with her. As soon as all the food is gone, she throws back her glass of wine and stands up.

Well, I'll be off then.

He lets her out. At the door, she suddenly says: Hmm, is it that girl from the train? The one you went to Paris with?

Max looks at her mockingly.

As if, she's barely old enough to be my daughter, my great-granddaughter, she's just helping me find my way in the new world.

Hmm, Madeleine says, then turns around. Well, see you later then, eh?

Only when he has slammed the door behind her does he notice how tense the encounter has made him. Suddenly, what she said about Paris hits him. Had he told her about that when they met? He's almost certain he hasn't.

...&...

Antoine had started with a short text message in his eye lens: Where are the Brederoo descendants these days? Do they still have any power? I found one of them in Switzerland, but some of them apparently live in the Peoples' Union as well.

He blinked and then saw: We have to go to Switzerland, Max.

He had replied with a spoken message. That he was very much considering stopping the search because they weren't getting anywhere anyway. The idea of travelling again also didn't sit well with him.

Then she had told him she was on her way over.

Antoine is wearing a weird pantsuit, a bit like a jumpsuit made from a fabric that appears to be somewhere halfway in between plastic and paper but is certainly neither. She has tied her hair into a tight bun. She's sporting pale pink sunglasses with sparkling frames, gold earrings in her ears and around her neck a necklace with a nugget of gold, shaped like an Easter Island statue.

My, don't you look different every day, says Max. What do you mean by that? she says sternly.

Nice. I think it's nice, he says hastily. I meant it as a compliment. I don't know much about fashion statements.

She sits down on his couch. I don't know which fashion statement you're talking about, I make my own clothes.

Max puts a glass of white wine in front of her. Gee, are we starting already? It's only four o'clock, she says.

Would you prefer water? Max asks and he picks up the glass again.

She snatches it from his hand and does it again, holding the wine up to the light, smelling it, gargling a little, then swallowing and inhaling oxygen to let the wine that was left on her tongue breathe before she tastes it.

Max looks at it with some amusement. Apparently, she really knows her stuff, because she mentions the grapes used and says they were grown here in the north on clay soil. He checks the label, she's right. She doesn't think much of it, by the way, he can tell by the tone of her voice.

She relaxes, presses her ear and calls out something. The big screen on the wall displays an image. It's a family tree, with the name Brederoo at the bottom. He looks at it intently, but Antoine clicks her tongue again and now the familiar image of John II appears.

It's possible to find out the whereabouts of all the Brederoos, she says, and whether or not they're still alive, except for this John II. So he may still be alive. But where?

Max laughs at her. Then he'd be 180 or so?

He was born in 1998 Max. He could be 127 years old.

2125 - THE HIBERNATOR

And you think he knows the true story, that he knows what happened to Felice? So why did he remain silent about this during the Paris Trials?

Well, I don't know. That is truly a mystery, Antoine says now. You don't seem very grateful, by the way. I'm trying to help you.

Max gets out of his chair and clinks his glass of wine against hers.

Sorry, Antoine. It's just that I get completely fed up with this story at times.

Fortunately, Felice isn't here this afternoon, Antoine says. She would get mad at you.

No, she definitely wouldn't. She thinks I should stop. And even so, her visits are just delusions, hallucinations, psychoses.

Antoine disagrees, it seems perfectly normal to me that someone keeps talking to you even after they're already gone. I lost my great love, my childhood sweetheart, just three years ago. I also still get regular visits. You must have a therapist who tells you you're talking to yourself?

Yes, how else would you know what Felice said during our trip? It was all me doing the talking. It all came out of my mouth.

Not true, Antoine says firmly. I also saw her Max.

And heard her.

You were stoned from those mushrooms.

No, I saw her. She wasn't really happy with me, I think. She called me 'that kid'.

Antoine gets up and walks to the fridge to see if there's anything left to eat. She grabs a container and puts it behind a little door in the device, where it gets warmed up in seconds. Max doesn't want anything. He likes to drink without eating, it makes the wine work better.

Antoine now shows him a name on the screen: John Brederoo III. Below it, there's an address in Lucerne.

We have to go pay this one a visit. And I also found the LDC headquarters. A castle in the Alps.

Just like that, Max says.

…&…

A taxi has dropped Max off at the border post, he has to walk the last bit. He envisions the Iron Curtain of yesteryear.

A strip of no man's land with a high, barbed-wire fence. In front and behind are bare strips of land where mines have been laid. Watch towers everywhere, with gun barrels sticking out. Soldiers patrolling and keeping an eye on everything. He knows that all of the 1,150 miles along the border look like this. Switzerland is a hermetically sealed collection of rocks, valleys, lakes, people and cows.

The fast train went no further than Lyon in France. Then he took a slightly slower train to a small French town that used to be almost intertwined with Geneva and is now separated by more than a hundred yards of land flattened by bulldozers. All to keep foreigners out of the independent mountain state.

The barrier opens after a man in uniform exited a small building and waved at it with a remote control. He indicates that Max should follow him inside. An officer with one star on his shoulder sits behind a table. He gives him a gruff look, stretches out his arms palms up, and Max places his folder, with the papers he picked up from the Swiss embassy, in them. The man gestures for him to sit down and starts reading without saying a word.

After 15 minutes, he finishes reading and says he wants to know the real reason for Max's visit. He thinks the whole story about his interest in mountains and lakes is bogus.

Don't think, says the officer gruffly, that we'll give you any leeway to spy on my country.

Max smiles kindly and says the man really has nothing to worry about, he loves the mountains of Switzerland.

A feeling of nostalgia overwhelms Max. Probably because of all the military parading around him. Customs officers who feel empowered by the uniform they wear, machine-gun nests with trigger-happy young men, an atmosphere of distrust and suspicion. But nostalgia or not, he also knows that he has always hated this kind of stuff.

The tram to central Geneva is full of grumpy-looking people; children, people on their way to work, greybeards staring out of the window with a bored look, everyone here looks as if Judgment Day has come and gone and the final verdict didn't turn out favorably for anyone here in Switzerland. He intrudes upon people for help because the signposts and other indications are in Swiss German, a language he doesn't understand. No one speaks English, everyone reacts sullenly or ignores him. Finally, with a humble pleading of 'bitte bitte' and a mispronounced name, he manages to get some directions on where to get off to reach his hotel.

He feels sorry for ever embarking on this trip. He thinks about home, his town, the trip to his island. To the kindness of everyone around him. A light-heartedness he finds very boring and corny at times, but which he now misses very much.

2125 - THE HIBERNATOR

He constantly has to dodge people on the street. They walk hunched over, peering at the pavement. Miraculously, they always narrowly manage to avoid collisions. They do constantly bump into him though. A well-run Swiss watch, in which he, as the outsider, is the irritating grain of sand that makes the whole mechanism grind to a halt.

The hotel, which he picked based on the photos and its reputation, turns out to be faded glory. Of its five stars, three have literally fallen off the facade, the building looks dilapidated.

The woman behind the reception desk has all the features of outward beauty from her Germanic origin, blonde hair and bright blue eyes, but her unfriendly attitude quickly negates them.

With a ferocious gesture, she slides his room key over to him.

He must pay in advance and pulls a stack of Swiss francs from his bag. A chip in your arm is useless here. He had to get a paper visa from the embassy and withdraw stacks of banknotes. Last week, he joked about how much he would enjoy returning to the normal old world, but he regrets it already.

The antique lift to the fifth floor stops working halfway up. At first, there is no response to the alarm bell he presses, and when someone finally appears after five minutes, he is met with a torrent of incomprehensible swear words, as if he has wrecked the lift himself. The door is wrenched open, and he struggles to pull himself up onto the floor that is five feet above him.

His room smells, the bed sheets haven't been changed. He walks down the stairs and, wordlessly miming his way through what he hopes is an explanation, tries in vain to plead that he wants clean sheets. The gruff woman doesn't speak a word of English, or doesn't want to, and she pretends not to understand his gestures.

He skulks off to the bar. He wants to drink himself to sleep because he knows the stench won't leave his room, even though he has opened the window wide.

Someone gestures for Max to join him, perhaps longing for some company. The man looks vaguely Asian; Max estimates him to be around 40. He wears a suit and tie. Max hasn't seen that useless piece of clothing anywhere since waking from his hibernation.

The man speaks English, his name is François Mitterrand and he's a businessman on a purchasing trip. He's from France, has heard of his famous namesake, but doesn't believe they're related.

The man is not at all interested in what Max is doing here. Nobody travels to the old world for fun, he claims, before lifting a pint of beer to his lips.

The Swiss didn't want to join the GUM, he says, and they're probably regretting that by now. But admitting that it was a stupid decision? No way. They used to have many underground resources here that are needed for the new energy industry. Rich finds in the 2060s. But well, now that everything is being reused in the free world, that market has dried up and no one wants old-fashioned timepieces anymore either.

François rattles on and on, and Max, by now with his own tankard of beer in front of him, feels himself fading. He's tired and not looking forward to the next day.

Why don't you just go home, says Felice. She drank from his beer and puts down his glass with a foam moustache under her nose. What are you doing here, in this miserable part of the world? I'm really not here anymore, Max darling.

Not anymore, so you have been here? He doesn't say it out loud, because that would interrupt François' monologue. He has lost track of what he's talking about by this time. He looks at Felice, she looks away.

Gotcha, Max thinks.

...&...

Max had seen the building from afar. It's at the top of the mountain and looks like a cross between a castle and a monastery, but most of it seems ruined. The road leading up to it is dilapidated, the tarmac is split, tree roots growing through it.

Shrubs and weeds grow in the cracks. According to a paper guidebook Max found in the hotel's library, this part of the Alps is an area for experienced hikers. A combination of stupidity and hubris has led him here. He opted for the asphalt road; the hiking trail from his guidebook leads past deep ravines, with steep descents and atrocious ascents. The tarmac road adds miles to the trip but is a lot more moderate. It's very quiet, he has been on the road for hours and hasn't seen a single person yet.

Arriving at the castle, he climbs the steps and walks through the hole where a door must once have been. Apart from a pair of pigeons cooing, the entrance hall is deadly quiet. He walks to the courtyard, which is enclosed by covered galleries. No sign of life anywhere. In the village, they told him that an eccentric figure lives here, who comes to the valley once a month on a moped to do some shopping. He calls himself 'the gatekeeper of the castle', but Max didn't see him at the gate. He has been warned that the man isn't very keen on visitors.

2125 - THE HIBERNATOR

Down a straight line from the main entrance, he sees another gate that leads to the back, where another building stands that must date from the 20th century, unlike the castle. It has many windows, but most of them are broken. Birds seem to be the only inhabitants. To the left of the building, there's something that looks like a caravan, overgrown by some kind of aggressive ivy.

Suddenly, he feels something cold on his neck. He turns and looks down the barrel of an M16, an automatic rifle that was very popular in many a war in his time. A burst from that thing would surely decapitate him. The weapon is in the hands of an old man who has such a frenzied look in his eyes that Max doesn't hesitate for a moment and disarms him with one quick move.

The gatekeeper stands there, stunned. Max himself is surprised by his quick action as well; he can't remember ever even being threatened with a gun, let alone disarming anyone. He greets the gatekeeper politely, introduces himself, says he comes from Holland South.

Holland South, the man repeats in amazement. Then he starts cursing and swearing in Swiss German. When Max apologizes politely in English, the man switches to that language without a hitch and continues swearing, in a thick American accent. What the fuck was Max thinking just walking in here and doesn't he fucking know this is private property. After another series of fucks, Max interrupts him, still in a friendly tone.

He says he's looking for the gatekeeper. The man's repertoire of bewildered facial expressions doesn't seem to be exhausted yet. He looks at Max with wide eyes but stops cursing.

For me? he stammers, then wants to know why the fuck that is?

I'm a historian, says Max, I'm interested in the history of this building.

Now something changes in the man's face, it relaxes. He introduces himself as Jack. His eyes remain focused on the rifle Max has under his arm, the barrel pointed towards the ground.

I know all about this place. But most of it is secret, so I can't tell you much.

Max walks with him to the caravan, a stuffy shack with the heater turned on high and a huge mess inside. There are clothes, food leftovers, dirty pots and pans everywhere. Max put the rifle outside against the caravan. Max pulls a bottle of good whisky from his backpack, which he sees Jack look at greedily.

Two weathered lemonade glasses arrive on the table, Max pours them full of a 30-year-old malt.

Jack talks about the importance of the castle in the world history. How all major inventions in the field of energy supply were once developed here. That it used to be a place where all the great geniuses of that industry came together to think about the future of mankind. Max lets him talk as much as possible because he notices Jack is keen to tell his story. Only when Jack starts repeating himself does he ask a question.

And the Lucerne Dredging Services, they were here too, right? he asks him when there's a brief silence.

He's so into his story that he confirms it enthusiastically at first, but a moment later he pretends to have never heard that name before.

The whisky really gets him going. By the fourth glass Max pours for him, Jack starts to lose track between the part of the history he's allowed to tell and the part he's not.

My father was a caretaker, he says. The best storyteller that ever existed in Switzerland. No, scratch that. The best in all of Europe, perhaps even the best in the world.

Max struggles to understand him because Jack has started to slur his words so much that it sounds as if he's lost control of his vowels. He calls himself his father's proud successor as the guardian of this historic site.

He lets slip that the LDS commandos have made the world a better place.

Max says: that's interesting. Do any of its archives still exist?

Archives? snorts Jack, everything here was all burnt long ago, he says, laughing aloud, I was there when my father set fire to it in the courtyard. Not long after, there was a raid by the international justice department.

They could root around in the ashes to their hearts' content but there was nothing left.

When Max asks Jack who pays him to be the caretaker here, Jack clams up. He looks at Max suspiciously and mutters that it's none of his business. The booze is slowly starting to cripple him. He leans back with his head against a cabinet.

That's none of your business, he mutters and drifts away for a moment.

A moment later, he starts talking again, largely unintelligible now. Max is breathing heavily. He hasn't had nearly as much whisky as Jack, and so is able to ask another question when the time is right. The key question, perhaps the only question that really matters to him. There are beads of sweat on his forehead.

Was there also a woman among the prisoners? he asks. Yes there were women too.

No, a specific one, a famous woman, an inventor and activist. It was world news at the time.

Oh that one yes, I think I do remember, Jack replies, glancing at the leftover whisky in the bottle Max is clasping. There were several women, but the one you're talking about, my father often mentioned her. That was so fucking secret, she was famous yes. Ha ha, the whole world was looking for her and there she was, just sitting here in the basement. I wasn't born yet, mind you. But my father told me everything.

Do you know what happened to her? Max hears his voice falter. He tries to control himself. He tries to sound casual when he asks: did she die here?

Ha, no, she was saved. My father told me eventually some hotshot came here and took her with him.

Someone from the Brederoo family?

Jack passes out for a moment, lets out a burp and tries to concentrate on the bottle again.

By a Brederoo? repeats Max.

I don't know, Jack mumbles and then passes out again.

...&...

He grabs a flashlight from the caravan table to go investigate. He can feel his pulse quicken. Jack is lying unconscious on the sofa. Max puts the bottle with the leftover malt on the floor beside him and wonders why he's doing this. He knows now, right? That Felice has been here?

But he wants to see it, up close.

He walks across the building's ground floor and finds a staircase leading down. There are many different rooms, all empty except for some overturned chairs, pieces of rubble or reinforced steel. What are the chances of him finding traces here of something that happened a century ago?

At the very back, he finds a long corridor with steel doors. He opens one and walks in. It's a cell. An old mattress lies on a concrete elevation. A stainless-steel toilet hangs on the wall, but that's all there is. Fresh air enters through an air duct. He sits down on the mattress.

Felice is there as well.

Congratulations, she says cynically. You found me! Wow, well done, Max. Look, this is the smelly mattress that I lay upon. Or was it in the cell next door? There was heating though. And that mattress didn't smell as bad as it does now. I got clean bedsheets every week. Look, that's the grate I tried to escape through, but it was too narrow. I'd already lost quite a bit of weight due to the disgusting food they served me, but I just didn't fit through.

Okay, so now you know. I was here. And? Now what, Max? Are you going home now? Are you finally going to live a life without me?

I still have plenty of questions, Felice. Did they steal your invention here? Forced you to sign that weird document that Daan had to have invalidated by the judge? And then? Did they kill you? Or did somebody really come and take you away, as that jerk in the caravan claims?

Just go home, to your flat, your friends. Focus on Eve. She suits you just fine. Just believe me. No more rooting around in the past, it's over and done.

Max lies down on the mattress. Listens to the sounds of the night he hears through the air duct, feeling queasy from all the booze and commotion. He sinks into a deep sleep.

When he wakes up, he can't tell how long he's been out. Daylight falls through the duct, so it must've been at least a couple of hours. He feels pain everywhere and is nauseated.

Only after he gets up does he notice that the steel door is closed. He tries to open it, but it's locked, doesn't move an inch. Could that heavy door have locked by itself? Or did Jack lock him up? He gasps. The hatch in the door is open. Max calls out. Is anyone there? When there's no reply, he starts screaming for help, rattling the door, feeling as if he's going to hyperventilate. The flashlight has disappeared. Has Jack been here? That's the only possible answer, isn't it? The idea that Jack must have locked him in here relieves him a bit. At least that means someone on this earth knows he's here.

Two hours later, still nothing has happened. He has sat down on the mattress and is counting. Every time he reaches a hundred, he walks to the hatch and calls for help as loudly as he can.

Will they just let him die here?

There's no water in the toilet and the tap doesn't work either. When he thinks about how many days a person can go without water, his throat starts to constrict again, he tries to put that thought out of his mind.

Then he hears a roaring sound getting closer, he recognizes it, a helicopter. He climbs on the mattress in an attempt to hear more. It seems to be landing, roaring and howling, it's as if he can feel the wind blowing through the air duct. The engine is turned off. He can hear voices but doesn't understand what they're saying. The conversation is in Swiss German, one of the voices sounds like Jack's. Max realizes that if he can hear them, they must also be able to hear him. He shouts for help as loud as he can. The men interrupt their conversation and then continue in a whisper. One of them hisses, sounding angry.

Then the helicopter's engine starts again and not long after, he hears it take off and fly away from the castle, the sound slowly dying away.

Despondent, he sits down on the mattress and starts counting again. When he has reached one hundred again, he wants to make another cry of distress through the hatch but then hears footsteps in the corridor.

The key is turned in the lock three times and the door opens. It's Jack. He steps back and holds his rifle at the ready. Max's backpack is next to him on the floor. Jack kicks it towards him and points with the barrel of the gun in the direction of the exit.

Max grabs his backpack and starts walking without saying a word.

He would like to ask why he was locked up and who was in the helicopter but decides it's better to keep his mouth shut. Jack follows him, perhaps with his finger on the trigger, until they're through the gate and Max is on the tarmac road.

All Jack says is: and now get the fuck out of here.

As he begins his trek down the hill, Max walks the first stretch more or less backwards, as if this will help him avoid being shot in the back. But after about 50 yards, he sees that Jack has disappeared.

The trip down to the valley is faster than his trip up in every respect.

...&...

The barrier of the gated community remains closed. The taxi driver has turned to him to ask for instructions. The security guard in the small booth next to the barrier has told them that Max isn't allowed in without an appointment and there are no mentions of an appointment in his logbook. Max wants to speak to John Brederoo III, who, according to Antoine's detective work, must live here. The doorman dismisses his request to call him with an arrogant smirk. Max doesn't know what to do. Even though he gives it little probability that his mission will succeed, he gets out and sends the taxi away. It's at least an hour's walk back to town, but he won't give up now. He sits down on a boulder stretched across the side of the road and demonstratively crosses his arms. The guard ignores him.

After half an hour, Max is still there. Two people have joined the guard in the cramped security booth by now. The three men look over at their strange guest regularly and are apparently discussing the best way to get rid of him. They've made several phone calls as well with a very old-fashioned handset, still attached to the phone with a wire.

Then a car approaches. It looks like a police car but isn't. Two uniformed men get out, also trying to worm their way into the small booth before looking at him through the window.

Eventually, one of them comes out and addresses him. In terse English, he gets told to fuck off. The man doesn't look like someone with any authority in this play, he looks more like a muscle head with broad shoulders, more jaw than forehead. A bald Neanderthal.

Max politely asks what the man will do if he doesn't. Call the police because someone is on a public road?

The man disappears back into the booth. Apparently, this is the first time they've had to deal with something like this, as they're back on the phone. A few minutes later they come to pick him up, he can come with them.

Behind the barrier, Max feels very uncomfortable. He walks in between the Neanderthal and a man who appears even larger and dumber. Behind the booth, there's some sort of golf cart in which they take a seat.

The road affords beautiful views onto a lake which has many superyachts and sailboats on it. The lake is actually too small for these kinds of boats; if you were to line them up, you could reach the other side without getting wet.

The villas they drive past are perhaps even more imposing. But before he knows it, they've passed a gate with another guard and, after a few minutes, they drive up to a gaudy little castle. They are met by a butler in appropriate classic attire. He takes them to the terrace where 'sir' is expecting them.

You are a pain in my arse, Mr Flowerday, John III begins without any greeting. He turns out to be a spry octogenarian. Max tries to find any family resemblance to this man's father, John number II, but no one would describe this man as a retired playboy.

More of a potentate, a classic patrician, an asshole.

Mr Brederoo I assume, Max says politely.

That's right. I understand that you wanted to speak to me. I don't want to speak to you. But since you're rather, how shall I put it... pushy, I'll let you say what you've come to say. So you can leave me alone after that.

I'm actually looking for your father.

My father is dead, says John III. What makes you think he's still alive? My father was born in 1998 and...

He would be 127, I know it's old, but there are older people walking around on this planet, Max interrupts him. The crazy thing is: I can't seem to find anything about your father's death anywhere. He wasn't buried in your family tomb in Zurich.

That's a private matter. Perhaps the family feels he doesn't belong there because of his role in the Paris Trials, for example. His behaviour there has certainly not made him popular with the family. You've read his testimonies in Paris if I'm not mistaken?

How did you know that? Max asks, startled. He looks around, the two guards are standing at an appropriate distance but are keeping a sharp eye on him.

Oh let's say, I have my sources.

Max wants to ask who those sources are, but figures that won't get him much further. He came here to ask another question.

Perhaps your sources also know what happened to my wife?

John looks at him mockingly and slowly shakes his head. Is that what you've come here for? To ask if my family is behind your wife's disappearance? What a complete moron you must be to ask such a question. You and your silly little investigation here. I have to say you do have guts. Do you have any idea how powerful my family is?

I might as well have left you to die up there in the mountains.

Again, Max is startled.

You were in that helicopter? He's surprised that Brederoo actually implicates himself in Felice's disappearance with that. Listen, Brederoo. I'm not at all interested in you and your family. I want to know what happened to my wife. When did she die? How did she die? I know she was imprisoned in that castle of yours. It would be good of you if you can tell me how she died. Where she's buried, he starts.

John III's face turns red and he understands he'd better keep his mouth shut.

You're pathetic, Mr Flowerday. Please leave. I don't know anything about your wife. I conclude that your visit was entirely unnecessary.

John gestures to the guards that they can take Max away again.

Back in the hotel library, he finds a computer, quite a modern-looking thing, but it has a very old-fashioned wired mouse and keyboard. The home screen looks like a search engine and it shows an address bar.

He enters an address that should connect him to the new world. A chat window of sorts appears and he taps in an address. Not long after, a text from Antoine appears on the screen.

Max, where are you? Everyone is worried.

He writes back that he's in Switzerland and asks if she's angry that he went alone.

Stupid, insanely stupid, idiotic even is the response he gets. We did everything we could to track you down and there you are, just popping back up.

He gives her a brief account of the meeting with John III and asks her for new leads, addresses. Surely there must be more Brederoos living in this country. Before she replies, the screen goes black. When he gets up to see if he perhaps accidentally kicked the plug out of the socket, a man is standing behind him. In his hand is Max's backpack, full of his things by the looks of it. Did they clear out his room?

The man drops the bag on the ground and fills the doorway, showing him a pass with the word Polizei on it, but then withdrawing it so quickly that Max can't read his name or rank. Two other men appear behind him, uniformed and with a large pistol on their hip.

What's the problem? asks Max. Is that my bag? What does this mean?

You will be escorted to the border by these two gentlemen, the inspector says in broken English.

I have a valid visa for another whole week, Max says. He grabs the paper out of his back pocket and unfolds it.

That visa has been revoked, says the inspector, who snatches it out of his hands and demonstratively tears it up. According to your visa, you came here to enjoy some time in the wilderness.

That's right. I went out on some beautiful hikes in the mountains, says Max.

The man starts listing all the things he believes Max has done wrong. Illegal entering of private property, investigating residents, providing false information to customs. He's no longer welcome.

Max tries to object, but the inspector beckons the uniformed men and shoves the backpack in Max's direction with his foot.

...&...

Antoine is lying on his living room sofa. She's asleep when Max enters. He sits down on the coffee table and looks at her. Her eyelids indicate she's in REM sleep. She has a sweet, innocent face, her breath slowly whistles in and out past her lips. He wonders what she's dreaming about. Her eyes shoot back and forth restlessly and a frown creases her forehead. Her breathing hitches for a moment as well.

He thinks of Sam. She was equally intense. Is that why he gets on so well with Antoine? He's missing a daughter and she's his substitute. A child, someone to protect, to help with a future, just to be a father.

He calls to her, almost in a whisper, and watches her slip into a dream for a few seconds before she opens her eyes. She looks straight at him and grunts.

Are you watching me? How long have you been sitting there? she asks. Hours, Max lies. What did you dream about?

Pff, none of your business. I'm still mad at you, you know.

He'd already spoken to her when he was on the train home. She'd freaked out after the sudden disconnection and became terribly worried when she could no longer reach him. She went to his flat to wait and a worried Aïcha met her there. She'd contacted the police, approached the consulate in Geneva, but no one knew anything.

Antoine rubs the sleep from her eyes.

Max smiles, gets up and goes to take a shower. In the bedroom, he puts his laundry in the washing machine. Whites, fur, wool, linen and silk: it washes everything together, without water, he doesn't understand how.

He waits for Antoine to leave, just standing there in his underwear.

But she stays and crosses her arms.

Well? Antoine says very loudly and emphatically.

Well what? asks Max.

Shit Max, tell me what you found out.

He waits a moment before answering her. But then, as he stands there in his underpants, with his shoulders drooping, he tells her the whole story.

She didn't die there Antoine, he says finally, as far as I can gather, someone took her away from there. That Brederoo guy wouldn't tell me anything, I was expelled from the country.

Silently she looks at him and then says impatiently: so now what?

Now nothing, Antoine. Don't you understand? It's over. Done. I quit. After these words, Max lowers his shoulders even further and then blows out all his tension in a protracted sigh.

I don't know why you say that. This story is far from over Max.

...&...

Madeleine is at the door of his flat again. Antoine, who spent the night on his sofa, opens the door for her, barefoot, with unkempt hair and sleep still in her eyes. She and Max had gotten drunk and he'd put her on the sofa and given her his duvet.

Madeleine walks past her, exactly as she did the first time with Max, without a word, straight into the living room. She plunks her handbag down on the coffee table.

And who are you? she asks over her shoulder in an unfriendly tone.

As Antoine only continues to stare at her in amazement, Madeleine turns to Max.

Well, aren't you going to introduce us? Her animosity is almost tangible. Hello Madeleine, how are you? This is Antoine, a good friend of mine. She's helping me with my research. Antoine, this is Madeleine, you saw her on the train the first time we met.

Madeleine takes another good look at Antoine.

Ah, right, the little Protestant. Your pint-sized travel assistant. She sits down in Max's chair and puts her feet on the coffee table, asks if they've had breakfast yet. They have and Max asks if she would like a croissant and some coffee.

Why not, she says gruffly.

Antoine sits down on the sofa opposite her.

Your hair is beautiful, really gorgeous, says Antoine with complete sincerity.

Madeleine looks at her a bit dumbfounded, fidgets with her long blonde locks briefly and seems to be momentarily thrown.

Well, your hair doesn't look bad either, says Madeleine, but sounds a lot less sincere. She asks if Antoine has been able to help Max with his 'Quest for the Dead Wife' yet.

Antoine says she thinks that sounds rather shitty.

Madeleine changes her tone and mutters that she didn't mean it like that. She sighs and asks if they're close to identifying a culprit yet.

Certainly, says Antoine, more than one.

Really? responds Madeleine. She takes her feet off the table and sits up straight. Tell me, she insists.

We most certainly won't, Max says before Antoine can continue.

Madeleine looks at him offended and asks why not. Don't you trust me? she asks.

It's a secret, says Antoine, understanding. Why are you so interested?

2125 - THE HIBERNATOR

Well, it has certainly been one of the biggest scandals of the last century. Where has Felice Ricci gone? So why do I want to know? Just out of compassionate curiosity, Madeleine snaps.

But then you'll also understand that we can't talk about it to just anyone, says Antoine.

But I'm not just anyone, am I? asks Madeleine, but it sounds more like a statement. She looks at Max almost pleadingly.

He shrugs and walks back to the kitchen with Antoine's empty cup to make her another latte.

After Madeleine's remark, it remains quiet in the living room for a while.

What do you do for a living Madeleine? Antoine then asks. Madeleine replies matter-of-factly: I work as a freelance business consultant.

Large businesses, small businesses? Which sectors? Antoine wants to know. Technology, food, retail? And what do you advise on?

Madeleine is taken aback by all of Antoine's questions. Well, a little bit of everything. Large, small, any sector, mainly about labor issues.

Even when asked what she's currently working on, there's another vague story about a factory and how all the people working there are unhappy, that she's doing research and making recommendations for the management. Antoine wants to know which factory that is.

Madeleine says it's a small business which Antoine has probably never heard of.

Madeleine's vagueness and her way of talking seem to have triggered Antoine.

So what did you find out?

What do you mean? asks Madeleine clearly irritated.

You know, about why the people in that small business are unhappy?

Really, Madeleine replies with something midway between a growl and a sigh, but she leaves it at that.

Max listened to it all while he was busy making the coffee. At first, he thinks it's all pretty funny, the way Antoine interrogates her. But it only increases his distrust of Madeleine. He can't figure out why this woman is interested in Felice, in her disappearance, in him, yes especially in him.

Well, are you ladies done chatting? Then it's time to open the wine. Madeleine says she has another appointment and has to go.

...&...

Max sits on his balcony and stares at the park below him. Antoine comes up behind him.

That Madeleine, she says, I don't trust her at all. I think she's stalking you for a reason, that there's something behind it. I don't even believe that her sitting on that train across from us was a coincidence. And that she just happened to bump into you in the city, as you told me, what are the chances of that?

A reason... says Max. It isn't a question, more just a repetition of that word.

Yes, that she has a mission.

And what makes you think that?

Well, the way she acts towards you. A bit possessive, as if you were in a relationship with her. Even just the way she barges in here. Like this is her house or something. She's 110 years too young for me, Max jokes. Surely it isn't suspicious that someone likes me? In actual fact, what you're saying is: what's such a beautiful woman doing with such an ugly old guy?

Has she hinted at an intimate relationship yet?

Am I that unattractive, Antoine? he replies with another question.

No Max, you're quite an attractive man for your age, but she's not a good match for you at all. He feels himself growing an inch at those words.

Not a match? So what doesn't match?

She's the ambitious, shallow, mean-spirited type, cares a lot about appearances, and she's smart, vain, jealous, vicious too. In short, everything you're not.

I'm smart, aren't I? Max asks a bit crestfallen after the character sketch sinks in.

You're certainly smart, but she's more the cunning sort. And you're vain as well. And stubborn. And blunt. Any normal woman would've called it a day long ago. But to get back to Madeleine, what I find most suspicious about her: who, other than you, me and maybe your therapist, would care about your search for Felice? Has she asked about it before?

Yes, she has. I think it's weird that she keeps asking about it. But I still believe it's mostly me she's interested in.

I don't, is all Antoine says to that.

In the old days, Max says, there were people who saw conspiracies everywhere as well. They thought big companies were watching them, manipulating them and spreading viruses to reduce the world's population.

2125 - THE HIBERNATOR

And governments, he exclaims with enthusiasm, governments that oppressed the entire society with secret networks of paedophiles and occult nutjobs. You're nothing but a conspiracy theorist.

Depends on how you look at it Max, she says shrugging her shoulders, but then continues: have you checked out this Madeleine?

What do you mean by checked out?

Well, on The Net, on Somep.

Of course, he says proudly.

Antoine has flipped open a screen and calls out Madeleine's name and hometown. There appears to be only one Madeleine Verdun.

Don't you think it's weird that she doesn't have a photo on her Somep profile?

Well, no, mine doesn't have one either, in fact, I don't even have a real profile, he pronounces that last word like it's something that got stuck in his throat.

That's because you have a fossilised mind, Antoine grunts. No wonder you have so few friends. Have you ever contacted her through her Somep?

No, she's always the one contacting me. Or running into me, or kicking down my door, like she did just now.

Antoine presses the screen and the familiar ringtone sounds. A woman who looks nothing like Madeleine appears on screen. Antoine apologizes and asks if she knows Max Flowerday. No, she doesn't know anyone called Max and she's never been to Barcelona either.

Conspiracy theorist, moi? asks Antoine in a mocking tone after she disconnects.

...&...

Antoine is waiting for him downstairs at the building's exit. She's wearing a rough green fabric jacket, pointy boots and trousers made of a hard, shiny material that also looks unfamiliar to Max. He followed her advice and put on sturdy clothes, now he understands why. Antoine came by bike. One of the few things left, along with bicycles and kick scooters, that don't drive around entirely automatically.

He greets her a little hesitantly with his hand on his heart. She asks if he's scared on the back of a motorbike. He has to admit that he's never been on the back of a motorbike before, or on the front, for that matter.

Trust me, she says.

Do you ride motorbikes often? he asks.

No, this is the first time.

What?

Just kidding. I drive regularly. I occasionally borrow this one from another Protestant.

Max briefly hesitates, unsure whether or not he'll get on.

He gets a strange-looking helmet to put on. When she puts hers on, her voice automatically sounds through his earpiece. She gets on the bike, he sits on the back. She tells him to hold on tight. That's it, he hears when he puts his arms around her waist and presses himself firmly against her. Before he even realizes it, the machine takes off down the road.

They tear past all the self-driving cars, they automatically slow down or dodge them. The trip leads them right through the city and they rip onto an exit road at great speed. There are tall, thick trees on either side, shooting past in a tight, straight line approaching 125 miles per hour.

Antoine takes turns at an angle of fewer than 30 degrees. Max holds on for dear life until Antoine slows down a bit. She laughs.

I'll have sore muscles everywhere tomorrow, she says, you're almost squeezing me to death. Are you scared?

Not at all, he lies.

Along with some cars, they drive onto a ferry that will take them across the river. There's a boatman, but he's sitting in a comfortable little galley, watching a program on The Net. Everything runs automatically.

Don't they give out fines for speeding? Max wants to know.

Antoine laughs. Her bright blue eyes look mischievously in his direction.

Well, she says, all those systems were invented by humans, of course. And therefore, can be manipulated. That's also why we're now on our way to someone who knows his way around systems well. This bike is offline for a day due to repairs. It's in a so-called garage somewhere and the mileage will remain the same as yesterday.

Hah, hackers, Max exclaims, rebellion against all that automation. But if there are hackers, there's also crime, no? Or at least something against the ordinary. Tell me it's true.

Of course there's crime, Max.

Bad people, thugs, scum, revolutionaries, bullies, Max exclaims happily. And I thought we lived in a state of totalitarian dullness.

There is and always has been a tiny percentage of mankind that's rotten to the core, says Antoine. In your days, it was the super-rich, criminals and dictators. Only 0.1% of

2125 - THE HIBERNATOR

the total world population was really corrupt, but that was enough to fuck up the whole world. How many people were there when you went for your nap?

Eight billion? She makes some quick calculations. Eight million evil people out of a population with billions. They dragged a lot more people down with them, of course. Entire nations sometimes, by using propaganda and disinformation. The stupid people followed them. And often, it wasn't even the guys at the top, but rather their minions who were the rotten eggs. They knocked off the top of that black pyramid. The movement that did that is called ThinkAges. They did it peacefully, thanks to democracy. But that was also quickly abolished afterwards.

Yeah, yeah, Antoine, and here you are, pretending that all of history has been erased. You seem to know more about it than you care to admit.

Ha ha, I looked it up for you, grandpa.

Max wants to ask more, but the ferry has reached the other side and Antoine puts on her helmet. She's back on her bike quickly and hits the spot behind her with her flat hand.

Mo is a lanky man with dark frizzy hair and a slightly dopey gait. Max estimates him to be about 60 years old. His house is maybe just over 300 square feet. There's a seating area, a kitchenette, and a shower stall on one end, on the other there's a huge screen on the wall, divided into eight or nine smaller screens. A keyboard and a mouse are on the table, something Max had only previously seen in Switzerland.

Antoine explained that Mo used to work for GUM's Digital Development Department. He resigned when he had had enough of the whole indolent bunch there.

Antoine is lecturing him again: that department is responsible for all the hardware and software used by governments in all departments, districts and states. The organization has all the stored information from every citizen, company and institution. The key is guarded by a committee of a hundred wise people. They're drawn by lot from the total pool of all judges, clergy and administrators.

Only they can jointly decide whether to deviate from the protocols that protect people's freedoms and privacy. But of course, there are also people who constructed all those security measures and keys and Mo is one of them.

Antoine says it with a broad smile on her face. Now Max understands how it's possible that the bike, which brought them here with lightning speed, is still in a garage somewhere.

What do you want from these Brederoos? Mo asks gruffly. He invited them to take a seat at his dining table but didn't offer them anything to drink. Antoine gave him a quick pat on the head when they came in, he didn't accept Max's outstretched hand.

I want to visit them and ask some questions.

What kind of questions? Mo wants to know.

Personal questions.

No, no way, says Mo, irritated. I'm about to do something illegal here so I believe I have the right to know why I'm doing it, get it?

Antoine comes to his aid. He wants to know what happened to his wife Felice Ricci. She tells Mo the whole story. The abduction, the castle, Brederoo.

Mo takes a better look at Max.

You're Felice Ricci's husband? You're the Hibernator? At least Mo didn't call him the 'Doomsday Professor', Max thinks gratefully.

He nods with a sour smile.

Oh man, now *that* was a woman, if the stories about her are true.

Max is silent for a moment and then says dryly: yes, I've heard them.

Another silence, then they all start laughing. The ice is broken.

Mo explains that he doesn't want to break into the actual servers. He proudly says that he's one of the few people who could, but there are lines he won't cross.

People like these are also precisely the ones you won't find in the mainstream systems, he explains. Sometimes, they aren't residents of the Peoples' Union and therefore difficult to track down. But no one is untraceable. Not to me, anyway. His face beams proudly as he gets to work. He slides his mouse back and forth a bit and then starts rattling away on his keyboard like a madman.

Chapter 5

The waiter put their lunch on the table and is pouring them a glass of wine. Max remembers Eve's way of eating from their previous meeting. He watches intently as she prepares the first bite of her Salade Niçoise. She cuts the green lettuce, bell pepper and asparagus into small pieces and slides a bit of each onto her fork. Then she carefully pushes it through the fake-tuna sauce lying in the middle of her plate. Only then does the fork go to her mouth.

The restaurant's outdoor seating area is located on a large pontoon floating in a tributary of the river. It has some ramshackle benches and tables and every time a boat passes by, the wine in their glasses sways with the bow waves.

Tuna that never saw the sea, Max says cheerfully, watching Eve as she carefully and thoughtfully devours her salad. She closes her eyes for a moment to enjoy the taste, then she opens her eyes and looks in surprise into the eyes of the staring Max, who bends over his plate of green soup, caught off guard. He's trying to lose some more weight. He started to get a bit paunchy and is too vain to ignore it. Every morning, Ilse shows him the fastest way to becoming the fittest 150-year-old in Holland South by using weights.

How many hours do you work, Eve?

Why do you want to know?

I think you work way too much. People work 20-hour weeks nowadays. Any longer and it's considered anti-social, I gather. I can take over some of your patients.

Eve starts laughing and then looks at him to see if perhaps he's serious.

You're looking for a job?

What could I do? I figured I could get trained as a therapist. An old-fashioned talking one that is, but people still need those too, don't they? I feel like I need to do something, but what can I do? On the other hand, why should I? He sums up: work, spend some of your free time, eat, sleep and then do that 365 times for another 42 years before drawing my last breath at the age of one hundred.

Two hundred, Eve corrects.

You sound like Ilse, he says and sighs deeply.

Are you getting depressed again, Max?

No, you see, it used to be all about belief, you had ambition, you wanted to believe that you could be somebody, get a career, succeed, achieve your goals and make money, you believed in money and more money, and buying stuff, more stuff, more stuff; every success you achieved strengthened your belief that you could beat anyone in the world. Sex, more sex, lots of sex. In the deeper sense, life revolved around sex and procreation, for men it was mainly lust and for women procreation. And if earthly things weren't enough to satisfy you, there would be a church, a party or a sect to present you with things you could start believing in.

Eve picks up the bottle of wine, fiddles with her finger at the residue of the wax that sealed the cork. She refills the glasses and hands one to Max. He holds it up to the light, it's a cloudy natural wine. She clinks her glass against his.

Only then does she answer him. A lot seems to have changed, but maybe not all that much, she says. Owning things has indeed become less important, there's a more equal distribution, accumulating extremely large amounts of money and property has become much harder. But why should you want to? You no longer have to own things, you rent something until you're tired of it. Very few people are still impressed by luxury items. Getting a promotion is more or less a given, as company structures have also changed. Companies now partly belong to the people who work there. The higher you climb onto that ladder, the more accountable you are, the more you earn and the more tax you pay. In your time, people worked themselves to death, now they'll think twice about that. Someone who's overly attached to wealth and possessions is seen as a bit... pathetic. The world has become more equal and just, other things are more important.

Such as? asks Max.

Love, she says without a second thought.

Max sees that Eve surprised herself with that statement. She wants to add something else, probably that French Revolution stuff again, but Max interrupts her before she does.

Yes, let's talk about that. Our love.

2125 - THE HIBERNATOR

You know I didn't mean that. You have your family, Aïcha, Felice, Simon, Maxim. You have friends like Madeleine, Antoine and Leonardo. So many people around you, so much love. You just haven't realized yet that they're the purpose of your life.

You deliberately don't mention yourself? asks Max disappointed.

Yes, no... Sorry, of course I'm also one of those people. I have to get used to not being your therapist anymore.

So you love me as well? he asks. Eve sighs deeply.

Yes, Max, she says, I love you as well.

Is there any chance you'll also fall in love with me? he asks.

Eve almost chokes on her wine.

Well, I don't know, she says when her mouth is empty again. Falling in love is really nothing but a momentary lapse of reason. A lovely one though, says Max. Because I'm quite sure I have fallen in love with you, Eve. You're such an amazing person Eve, so beautiful, sweet, elegant and incredibly erudite. I know you think I just see another Felice in you. But you're different than she was. She was also beautiful, but in a different way, and yes, she was erudite as well, of course. But not as sweet as you, she could be quite nasty at times.

I can be nasty too, you know, Eve says, somewhat crestfallen. Max can tell that she immediately regrets saying that. She searches for words, avoiding his eyes while she does so.

He grabs her hand, her fork falls onto her plate. He's surprised that she doesn't withdraw her hand, she even turns it around and kind of grabs onto his. He looks at her mouth again, there's a faint smile on her lips.

I think you're a very nice person, Max. Really. And I do love you in a special way. But I closed the love chapter years ago.

Max smiles. Very good, Eve. You have to close a chapter to start a new one. I also finished the Felice chapter. And I want to start the next chapter. With you.

Eve stares at their hands.

I have thought about it Max, she says. But I'm just not the right partner for you. You're an adventurer, a doer, big, strong, easily bored. You are a traveler, a time traveler, stuck in the past. I'm only rooted in the present, I lead a very moderate life and I try to avoid an overabundance of stimuli. I stay in one place, hardly leave my house. The only variety is provided by my clients and their stories, although they also all kind of boil down to the same thing. Well, except yours perhaps.

Max rubs his thumb in her palm without letting go of her hand. He feels her answering the caress with her thumb, she bows her head, not looking at him.

A boat passes by with some teenagers on it. Music sounds from somewhere near the bow and the girls and boys are bobbing along merrily. The small boat rocks back and forth precariously. A girl looks over and waves one hand at him while using the other one to put a bottle to her mouth.

We're still young, says Max as he waves back with his free hand. I'm only just over halfway through my life and you're not even there yet. He grabs her other hand. Give it a chance, Eve. I love the idea of being with you so much. Teach me to do nothing. Teach me to live moderately. Then I will teach you to enjoy adventure.

Max stands up, sits down next to her and slowly leans in towards her. Just before his lips touch hers, he stops. He feels her breath on his face, it seems like an eternity passes before she closes those last few inches he has left open.

The kiss lasts forever for Max, but in reality it's over quickly.

Let's not rush it, says Eve as she lets go of him and turns her face away.

...&...

A mountain ridge has been raised along the North Sea coast. Millions of cubic feet of sand cover a huge concrete embankment. Beachgrass and sea buckthorn keep the sand in place. From the car park, it looks like a ridge of ancient dunes.

Max climbs to the top of the raised dunes via a network of wooden stairs and footbridges. When he reaches the top, he sees giant wooden decks, floating in the sea. They move with the tide, sliding up and down along a bare concrete quay. The floating platforms are about 300 by 100 feet. There are dozens of them, as far as the eye can see. The beach from his time must be far beneath where they now float.

People put down their towels or rented a beach chair with an umbrella on the wooden floor, in which sand pits have been constructed. Each platform has a small bar selling drinks and snacks. He, Aïcha and little Felice manage to find one of the last spots.

New land has been reclaimed less than half a mile from the coast. Wadden islands, overgrown with forests, with an endless number of wind turbines towering above the trees. Not with blades like they used to have, they're helix-shaped behemoths almost 500 feet high.

2125 - THE HIBERNATOR

The islands block the tidal waves that the regularly occurring mega-storms whip up, Aïcha explains. About 80 years ago, they obliterated the dunes and flooded the hinterland.

Aïcha and Felice change clothes, without fuss, without embarrassment. They both put on swimming shorts and walk to the edge of the deck to dive into the sea. Max slumps down in his chair, not intending to even take off his shoes. It's all joy and merriment here, families, groups of friends or couples enjoying the spring sunshine. He has heard that the sea level has stopped rising. Climate change has been reversed and after the last big blow, when a piece of ice the size of France broke off from the South Pole, sea levels didn't rise any further.

By the time Aïcha and Felice return, Max has fetched water and ice creams, they guzzle it all down greedily. After Aïcha emerges from the sea and lies down in the sun to dry herself, Max can begin the conversation that was the actual reason for him to join them here at the beach.

I really need to stop looking for Felice now, he tells her, I just about know what happened to her. In fact, I have strong indications of who was behind it. But what's the point of finding out every detail? The people responsible are certainly dead.

Aïcha stands up, places an ice cube in her mouth, puts a water bottle to her lips and lets the liquid flow past the cube, into her mouth.

So what's your story now? she asks. Are you really at peace with it?

I still have to guess as to what happened exactly. But Felice certainly didn't give away the patent, she didn't let them bribe her. She was imprisoned in a Swiss castle and was probably murdered elsewhere. All because of that damn invention.

But can you stop if you're still not sure? asks Aïcha. He can tell that she doesn't believe him. It's so unlike you to give up now.

I have to, says Max. I want to start a relationship with someone and all that stuff with Felice is getting in the way.

What? Aïcha exclaims enthusiastically. Really Max? With whom? Anyone I know? It's not Eve, is it? Oh, please let it be Eve. She's amazing!

Yes, Aïcha. I honestly think she's a very special woman. She's, she's, so...

And will it work out? I mean does she like you too? asks Aïcha.

I don't know, she says she needs time. She doesn't want to rush it. I'm not really sure how to proceed now.

I know her. She's been disappointed in love too often, she says. Take it easy. Let her get used to the idea. Pamper her. I'll go and visit her later this week, see if I can help in any way.

Ha ha, Aïcha's going to hook me up, Max chuckles. Gosh, these things used to be a lot easier. You got yourself a date, went out to dinner, maybe a little dancing after that, then back home for some more wine and into the bedroom you went.

Pff, says Aïcha, I shudder to think.

...&...

Antoine on the phone. She talks loudly, her voice rasping distortedly from Max's living room wall.

I've got her, Max! she shouts and waits a moment for his response. Mo was right, she has a completely different name.

Antoine tries to maneuver the camera in the right position for her video connection with Max.

You'll never guess her real name, she continues.

Not a clue, Max mutters. He hesitated briefly whether he should answer the call or just ignore it. It's late, he's lying on his sofa watching a film from 1998, the year his son Daan was born. Armageddon, a film version that somehow made it through the DataFade. He loved that kind of Doomsday movie. But he knew Antoine would keep trying until she got a hold of him.

Just tell me, sounds like I won't be able to guess anyway.

Magdalena Brederoo! Her voice falters and the emotion makes her breathless.

Max looks at her through the screen with a dazed look. Excuse me, Brederoo? Are you quite sure? he asks.

Max sees the look she gives him, proud as a peacock.

She's a spy, Mr. conspiracy denier. She's been watching you all this time for that Brederoo guy.

That Brederoo guy? asks Max, which one do you mean?

How the hell should I know? Didn't that Brederoo in Switzerland say he had his sources?

No, no way. She can't be working for that bastard, can she? We're going to confront her together, aren't we? I want to be there. I'll send you some info on your message board.

2125 - THE HIBERNATOR

He feels the adrenaline racing through his blood after he disconnects. He gets up and decides on a course to use for his pacing.

It works a treat, back and forth in a firm stride. His strides propel the blood through his thighs, calves and feet and he disappears into his meditative void. Counting, this many steps out, this many steps back. He can almost do it with his eyes closed.

But then he gives in and asks Ilse to open his message board. Standing in front of his screen, he sees a large picture of Madeleine. It's some kind of official portrait. She's wearing an evening gown and looks straight into the lens. Below the picture is her full name. Magdalena Johanna Frederica Brederoo. He knows that if he clicks on the name, he'll get a direct connection to her. He briefly thinks about resuming his pacing but then calls her anyway. The ringing tone sounds loudly through the room.

Then Madeleine appears on screen, visibly startles when she recognizes Max and disconnects.

Max tries again, but there's no answer this time. A screen appears, asking him to leave a message.

Felice enters the room.

Ha ha, that's what you get. I warned you about that woman.

That's exactly what you didn't do, says Max. You didn't warn me about anything. You just let me muddle along endlessly instead of just telling me the whole story.

He has a very clear picture of her. She wears her simple black dress, pumps on her feet and has her hair tied up high in a bun. She stands where he can't pace around her, her face like a thundercloud. He wants to yell at her to go away, but he's actually also pretty glad she showed up again. Trying to avoid her, he walks to the terrace and opens the door to the outside. The fresh evening air gives him some space to breathe again. His chest feels like a truck just ran over it.

Felice follows him outside.

I'm not telling you anything because I'm you, Max. You know that. I'll never know more than you because I just don't exist anymore. That's all. Go do something useful with your life, man.

Damn, you sound like my mother. Go do something useful Max, he imitates her, puts his head in his hands. It has to end, Felice. I love you, but I just can't go on if you keep haunting me like this.

Okay, so I take it I can finally say goodbye to you?

Oh no. Like in one of those bad films where the apparition suddenly disappears and crosses over to the other side, he says, in an attempt to be funny.

But he sees her face and attitude change. A huge sadness suddenly appears in her eyes. He swallows, at a loss for words.

She stands right in front of him and looks at him again. Places two fingers on her mouth, sending a kiss in his direction. Then she suddenly vanishes.

The space around Max is very quiet suddenly. He has trouble breathing, gasps for breath. His heart rate jumps up in a flash. He gets lightheaded, scared, starts hyperventilating. He gets down on all fours looking for something to breathe into and when he finds it and slowly recovers his breath, starts crying softly.

...&...

The bell rings. Ilse says Madeleine is at the door. Indeed, he sees her peering into the camera, and he opens the door without speaking. His heart is beating rapidly.

In front of his flat door, he keeps her waiting. When he opens it, she storms in. Swearing, sighing and slightly out of breath, she drops into Max's chair. He asks if she wants a drink. She does because she understands that he now knows the truth. That she lied about her name and all that. So she needs a big measure of the strongest drink he has.

Max takes his time as he goes to get a bottle from the freezer, a bottle he got from Leonardo. Irish Sunshine with the impossibly high alcohol content. He pours a full glass and hands it to her.

She takes one big gulp and her face cramps up. She does her best to pretend she isn't almost choking.

You probably want to know everything, right? she says when she has calmed down somewhat.

What do you think, Madeleine? Or should I say Magdalena?

No, that's my official name, Madeleine is what people call me, she says irritably.

Then at least one thing that you said was true. And you're in touch with that nasty John III, whom I met in Switzerland. Is that your father?

No, my grandfather. A terrible man. I did it for my father. She sighs, shakes her head wildly and adds: you must find it all pretty implausible. Max stays mute. He looks at her mockingly, as if to say: I don't give a damn about what you want to say to me.

She begins her story. Her father is in the district parliament. He had shown her Max's interview on The Net and told her this was bad news for him. He wouldn't stand a chance to be drawn for a post in Madrid in the GUM government if Max started prying into his family's activities. And that was certainly possible, her father had said.

I told him there was little we could do about it, Madeleine says, but he asked me if I could discreetly gather some information about you. He wanted to know what you retained from the past. What you would remember again. Who you would suspect of the disappearance, perhaps his grandfather John II? I did it for my father. So no bad intentions, really. I did find it exciting and besides, my interest in you grew when I realized you were more interesting and much nicer than expected. I mean it, she adds as Max looks at her with a raised eyebrow.

She sighs deeply, takes another sip of the Sunshine and then another.

Just as I wanted to approach you, you were leaving for the Balearics and my father made up some excuse for me to go to Catalonia. Back on the train from Barcelona, I managed to reserve a seat opposite you. I just wanted to befriend you. And try to pry some information out of you. That's really all it was, Max. He hasn't spoken yet, thinking of Antoine, who'll probably be angry that she isn't here right now.

Perhaps he should've waited before he called her.

So your father is John IV? And John II took his secrets to the grave with him.

Madeleine looks at him piercingly for a moment. My great-grandfather is still alive, she says solemnly.

Max freezes, his jaw drops. Excuse me?

But he's 127, very old and unfortunately very confused. Can I speak to him? I want to speak to him.

I think you should talk to my father first, no one gets access to John II without his permission. He's very protective when it comes to his grandfather.

Shit Madeleine, I've kind of had it with you. You really are bad news. He says it harshly and unkindly. You don't think it's all that bad, but we're talking about murder here. A murder from a century ago, but still...

Madeleine immediately starts crying. It's not just crying, it's a huge crying fit, with long outbursts, jerky breathing and lots of noise.

Max hesitates to go to her and comfort her. Clearly, that's what she wants. She looks at him questioningly between sobs. Eventually, he does get up and sits down opposite her with his hands on her shoulders.

Well, he sighs, at least now we know a little more. Just give me your father's address.

His consoling gesture doesn't help much, because now the sobs are intermittently interrupted by her attempts to communicate. She can understand that he has totally had it with her but that she really isn't a bad person.

He calmly goes to fetch her a glass of water and when he returns, she has calmed down a little.

They face each other silently for a while. Max has handed her a white cotton handkerchief and wonders if he'll still be able to wash out the black mascara smudges currently being rubbed into it. Around her eyes are broad black circles, with two red-rimmed orbs at their center. He wants to say something about clown-like appearances but wisely keeps his mouth shut when she gets up to go to the toilet. He patiently waits for her to return. She removed the makeup completely. Now the entire area around her eyes and mouth is red from rubbing.

She isn't leaving. The Sunshine from Ireland is going down smoother and smoother. Her sentences become increasingly incoherent and when he wants to order a taxi, she starts crying again. She gets up one more time to go to the toilet and drops down into the sofa when she returns, leaning against Max. She touches him, tries to hug him, but he gets up. Then she lies down and falls asleep almost immediately. He takes off her shoes and puts her on the sofa. She drifts off into a comatose sleep. He covers her with a blanket.

When he wakes up the next day and walks into the room, she has disappeared.

...&...

Max has cooked for her. A salad with artichoke hearts, dried tomatoes and smoked nut cheese, followed by a main course of sweet potato fries, grilled eggplant topped with mushrooms and wild asparagus. For dessert, peaches and liqueur ice cream, made in his new ice cream machine. He got one because little Felice was eager to make ice cream with him.

I'm really sorry, he says as they dig into the ice cream. But I couldn't resist calling her. She disconnected immediately, but an hour later she was at my door.

Sure, Antoine says, curtly. You keep doing that. Arranging and figuring things out on your own. We were in this together, weren't we? You keep doing this, suddenly leaving me out.

No, Antoine, this is really my own struggle, my problem, my quest. I'm really incredibly grateful that you've been helping me. Indeed, I wouldn't have come this far without you, but I have to finish this myself.

She ignores him, looks angry, wolfs down her ice cream until she suddenly makes an odd face and pushes her thumb against her palate. Brain freeze!

Madeleine came here to cry on my shoulder, Max says, dramas, tears, apologies. So I just forgave her. She did it for her father.

The brain freeze apparently melts away immediately, burnt down by a flaming rage that ignited in Antoine. Straight away, she's all 'bitch this' and 'bitch that'. What do you mean forgiven? A spy, a traitor, a slut who had lied to him to protect her family's honor.

Max's initial gratefulness that at least she's not crying, soon evaporates. Tears are streaming down Antoine's cheeks. Good thing she's not wearing mascara, flashes through his mind. He gets up and pulls her out of her chair, puts his arms around her and tries to say something comforting.

Come on Antoine, you helped me reveal the secret of the century. Well, from the last century at least. And despite the lack of history and decent archives, we have uncovered most of the mystery surrounding Felice. Too bad no one except for me is interested, but that doesn't make me any less grateful.

I'm interested in it too, she sputters back at him.

...&...

He's been waiting in the park opposite John IV's house for an hour and a half. Madeleine hadn't been able to persuade her father to meet Max, though she had gone against his express wish and given him his address. The man lives in a simple house with several bells at the front door.

Madeleine also told him that her father walks his beloved dachshund Bella in the park every day. The wait is long, but Max is rather enjoying himself. The weather is nice and lots of beautiful people walk by. He loves people-watching. He used to do that with Felice. They discussed the women Max thought beautiful, and she commented on the fashion statements that paraded past. He was having a hard time looking at the street scenes in the same way now. Men and women are equally beautiful, elegant or sexy or the exact opposite, and he can't make head nor tail of the fashion at all.

Then John IV steps out of his house with Bella. Max immediately knows it's him. Not because of the little dog Madeleine described, but because of the resemblance to his grandfather. John IV is a big man with the jawline of his grandfather John II. He strides along confidently, while the comparatively little dog on its leash happily scurries out in front of him.

Once he has passed Max's bench, he sets off in pursuit at a good distance. They pass some statues, a pond and a beautiful Art Deco-style recreated winter garden, where the exotic plants push against the glass as if they're trying to escape. Brederoo chooses a bench opposite a large pond, Max grins contentedly.

He has been practicing his speech, reckons Brederoo will try to walk away immediately, but he's determined not to let that happen.

As he sits down, John IV taps the brim of his hat with two fingers and mutters a greeting. Max greets back and bends over the little dog he lures with a click of his tongue. The creature approaches him with interest.

My name is Max Flowerday, Max then says, sitting back up, I know from your daughter Madeleine that you prefer not to speak to me, but it's very important to me that you do.

Brederoo looks as if he's watching the pond catch fire, pulls Bella towards him and begins to stand up. But Max stretches out his arm in front of him.

You can walk away but it'll be useless. I won't leave you alone until you tell me what you know about my wife, Felice Ricci. I will continue to stalk you, not just here on the street or at your front door, but wherever you may go. I will continue to pursue your father whenever he comes to the Union, search your family's history, file a lawsuit against you for violating my privacy by having me spied on.

Brederoo now looks at Max as if he's choking on something, tries to regain his breath and then hunches over slightly. He's apparently trying to process the threats Max has thrown at him.

You are very rude and aggressive, John IV finally says in a thin voice.

You know my history, Max says immediately. Your family history, yours or your father's, doesn't interest me. But I feel I have a right to know what happened to my wife, however long ago it was. I'm sorry for coming across as aggressive.

Brederoo reflects and Max grants him time to do so. People pass, little dogs sniff the dachshund, minutes go by without anything happening. Max's heart is beating wildly.

You should know, Brederoo begins, that my lot has been drawn to become secretary-general at the Justice Department in Madrid. I've studied for that. In no way have I ever been involved in my family's interests, and especially never in my father's business. My entire life has been dedicated to the common good. I climbed through the ranks as a civil servant in this district for decades and eventually entered the district parliament. I'm now working for the governor's office and as a result, my name has been drawn for a post in the central government. If you rake up my whole nasty family history again, it could have disastrous consequences for my mission. People at the GUM are quite allergic to stories like this.

Your career doesn't interest me at all, Max interrupts him. I want to know what your family did to my wife. I know there's a complicated story behind this whole affair.

My father never wanted to tell me, we've fallen out. My grandfather John II, with whom I do still have a good relationship, also never told me the family secrets regarding Global Energy. I wonder if your suspicions are correct. Apart from that, I just wanted to know if your research would lead you to start rooting around in our history. I was afraid of the publicity, the risk to my grandfather's good name, everything. I saw the interview with you and I... I panicked. I know you don't care about my feelings, but I'm telling it like it is.

Max nods impatiently.

Brederoo pauses for a moment and then says: the worst part is that I really don't know anything about the affair you're investigating. A brief silence before he continues: I only asked Madeleine to find out how you came out of this so-called coma to assess what to do next with this situation. How your brain, your memory, was affected, or whether you came out of it unscathed. She took that task quite seriously and threw herself into it with everything she had. Very awkward, very unfortunate.

So you don't know anything? asks Max disappointedly, ignoring the whole affair with Madeleine. Your father or grandfather never said anything about Felice Ricci?

All they ever said was that it was something we'd better never speak of again. I never asked any further.

But your grandfather is still alive and he knows. I want to speak to him.

That'll be very difficult. He's very old and his memory has largely disappeared. It won't be long before he dies. I'm afraid I can't allow it.

I don't believe I care a whole lot about getting your permission to visit him.

...&...

The apartment complex is located by the sea and Max walks up a wide avenue to get to the front door. There are some shiny vintage cars in a small car park, but it doesn't look like they ever leave it. Max enjoys looking at this small exhibition from the days of yore.

The reception area is overly luxurious. Sumptuous in a way that is now extinct: shiny copper doorknobs, sleek teak parquet floors polished into a glassy sheen. Persian carpets so tight it seems like they were knotted yesterday. Behind the counter is a friendly doorman with headphones. He contacts John Brederoo II's flat at Max's request.

Mr Brederoo would like to know what it is regarding? he asks after some time.

About Felice Ricci. I have a few questions for Mr Brederoo about my wife Felice Ricci, he says loudly, hoping the party on the other side can hear.

Carefully, the man repeats Max's remark to the person on the phone, judging by his choice of words, it isn't Brederoo himself.

Mrs Van der Beken Pasteel will come to see you in a moment, the doorman tells him.

That sounds classy, Max thinks, and she confirms that as she strides down the stairs a moment later. She is about 70, with many wrinkles, a thin mouth, and is ornamented head to hands in gold and precious stones, swathed in a classic dress with white lace trim. She announces her full title with Nina preceding it and asks what she can do for him. Max explains who he is and what he came here for.

Mr Flowerday, I'm afraid you're in for a disappointment. Mr Brederoo is very old and suffered a brain haemorrhage several years ago. His memory has been severely impacted by it. So he can't really aid you in your search. Perhaps I can help you?

Max reacts angrily. He wants to speak to Brederoo himself, says he will be gentle with him. Van der Beken Pasteel eyes him with a meaningful look that Max has trouble interpreting. He takes a step in her direction.

She says: very well, if you insist, Mr Flowerday, please follow me. She turns and strides up the stairs.

John II sits at the window in a huge armchair, there isn't much left of the big strong man Max saw in his pictures. When he met Felice, he was a muscular playboy with a tanned face and a remarkably unblemished row of white teeth. Now he's as thin as a rake, his hands are trembling and clearly, he has shrunk in size considerably. Only his teeth are still the same, but now slightly oversized in the sunken face.

Hello, junior, he says kindly, did you bring me any chocolate? Hide it from Nina if you did, because she keeps stealing it from right under my nose. With that sweet tooth of hers.

I'm Max Flowerday, says Max.

Don't confuse me John, he says and his thoughts stray for a moment. Then he looks at Max piercingly with suspicion in his eyes.

Do I know you? You look familiar, have we met before?

You don't know me, I'm here with a question. A question about the past.

2125 - THE HIBERNATOR

There's nothing wrong with my memory, John. Boy, you can ask me anything. You know that, right? That you can always ask me anything?

Nina is watching the whole thing from a distance. She shakes her head, wants to say something, but then decides against it.

Felice Ricci, says Max, you met her in Dubai, she came to talk to you.

John drifts off again. His head has tilted to the side and his tongue is poking out slightly from the lowest corner of his mouth. Then he jerks up again and starts a discourse on the desert, sounding rather confused. He describes plants and talks about sand being the fuel for new energy.

Yes sand, among other things, was used in Felice's invention, Max says. Which your family tried to get the patent for. Felice was a beautiful woman. She came to visit you in Dubai. There was also a lot of sand there. You must remember her.

The man suddenly looks at him with anger in his eyes. Don't treat me like a child, sir. You think I don't know that there's a lot of sand in Dubai?

Max doesn't back off.

But do you remember Felice?

I remember everything, my entire life in every detail, he snaps at Max, and don't try to tell me that I don't.

So what happened to her? asks Max.

To whom? And who are you?

To Felice, her name was Felice and I'm Max Flowerday, he says dejectedly.

Nina has fetched Max a glass of water because he declined the offer of tea or coffee. She serves it with a chocolate on the side. Brederoo also gets something to drink. A glass of milk with his medicine and a chocolate. He gobbles it down eagerly as if afraid it'll be taken away from him.

They sit facing each other silently for a few more minutes, sipping the water and milk, chewing the dark chocolate. Nina tells him there's no use in staying and that John II is tired and ready for his afternoon nap.

Nina walks him out, and as he stands at the door after saying goodbye to Brederoo, John shouts something.

Felice is outside on the beach. She's not coming back, he says.

Max freezes for a moment but then walks hurriedly back into the room.

Excuse me, what did you say Mr Brederoo? he asks sternly. She was a wonderful woman, but she left. Onto the beach. And she's never coming back, John says. Then his head nods to the side and his breath hitches. As if he's taken his last breath right there and then.

Max waits, nothing happens. But just as he starts thinking about CPR, John suddenly takes a deep breath and snores loudly as he exhales.

Nina now approaches him and takes him by the arm, escorting him to the front door.

Wait for me downstairs, she whispers and pushes him out the door.

...&...

An anger that he can barely control has taken hold of him. He's angry at the world, angry at that dilapidated man who could expire at any moment, but also furious at himself for his foolish obsession with this hopeless mission.

The doorman still looks at him kindly as he waits in the foyer. Max paces down the hall with clenched fists as if he's about to smash into something at any moment.

Nina strides down the wide marble staircase again. She has put on a coat and draped a scarf around her head.

We're going for a walk, she says when she reaches Max.

The doorman rushes to the glass door to open it for them.

They walk into the park, which is next to the apartment complex. The vegetation is simple here, so close to the sea which sloshes against the concrete beach quay some 300 feet away. Beachgrass, buckthorn, conifers are pretty much the only vegetation, but they've all been planted with so much forethought that an engaging environment has been created. The occasional patch of lawn with some heath dog violets and crocuses that have survived the robotic lawnmower and a brackish pond with mangrove-like plants. A beautiful order in a rugged landscape.

They arrive at a small gazebo constructed with artfully shaped cast iron, a slate roof, an oak floor. There are two chairs and a small table, at which they sit down. Max waits tensely for Nina to start talking.

I started working for Mr Brederoo 45 years ago. I wasn't even 30 yet at the time. I started as his secretary and now I'm his companion.

Since his brain has started to deteriorate, I've been reluctant to leave his side. There's so much they can do these days, but certain damages are beyond repair.

She sighs deeply and looks at Max with a long and piercing look. I know your story, Mr Flowerday. I respect your dogged search for the truth. What I'm about to tell you is known to very few people and I hope you'll be prudent about this knowledge. I know I can't ask for that, but I ask you nonetheless. I am telling you this out of compassion. She pauses briefly again.

Max nods.

You are here thanks to John. My John, not all those other men with the same name. You should know, John is a good man, a virtuous man, which can't be said of many of his family members. In the 2060s, John got your coffin, thing, capsule, what shall I call it?

My... capsule, Max says hesitantly. He can hardly believe his ears.

Your capsule... John got it out of Mexico and paid the management at your city's hospital a sum of money for them to keep you alive there. That weird doctor's clinic in Mexico was about to go under and if he had left you there, you wouldn't be sitting here now. You should know, John had made a promise.

Made a promise? To whom? To Felice? Max almost starts to hyperventilate again, but Nina gestures for him to keep still. Actually, John wanted to tell you all this himself. That was also one of the reasons for your transport here. That Doctor Bustemente even gave him some medication for him to prolong his own life so he would still be able to speak to you. He promised himself that he would tell you the truth, should you stay alive and wake up in good health. He told me everything at a time when things were very bad for him.

It was a crisis he overcame again, but I promised him I would tell you what happened to your wife if he wouldn't be able to do so himself.

A gust of wind blows through the gazebo. As if Felice briefly stopped by to haunt the conversation.

Nina talks on.

John was initiated into the secrets of his family's business in 2024. This happened in a castle in Switzerland, where secret meetings of industry leaders took place and which also served as a base for illegal operations that were carried out. Your wife's disappearance was a big thing even then, you hadn't yet left for Mexico. John found your wife there in that castle, in a cell. I won't describe to you the condition she was in. I can only tell you that the criminals in that castle tried their hardest to break her and there was little left of the woman she must once have been. John personally took her away from there. A private undertaking, without his family's consent.

Nina pauses for a moment. The severe majesty in her face has now largely vanished. As if the story she's telling has wiped it away.

John looked after her, helped her get clean, rehabilitate. They made progress occasionally, but she would often regress completely due to another brain hemorrhage, the result of all the drugs they had tried out on her to try and break her. She was half paralyzed, unable to speak. She still responded, knew what was going on around her, but could no longer really communicate.

John didn't want to give up on her. Ever since their first meeting, just before her disappearance, he had developed a huge admiration for her. I used to call it a mother complex because, after all, she was 23 years his senior. He worshipped her and became truly obsessed with saving her. But your wife was powerless, unable to do anything without him and the nurses, doctors and therapists he hired.

Then came the news about you. About your incurable illness and subsequent disappearance.

Another silence. Max is on the edge of his seat.

He told her and she was devastated. One day, she too had disappeared, Nina continues. It was either suicide or an accident, we'll never know, but her body washed up on the shore a few days later. John was beside himself. He never really recovered from that event; despite his subsequent marriages, he called her the most important woman in his life.

Nina's head and shoulders sag and Max takes a deep breath, staring at her dejectedly.

Nina sighs deeply. She has unburdened herself. She delivered the message.

Max, by contrast, breathes in deeply, as if he had forgotten to breathe for a long time.

I will leave you alone now, says Nina. I'm so very sorry for you.

She stands up, bidding him farewell with her hand on her heart. Max wants to say something, to thank her, but the lump in his throat is so big that he has to say goodbye with a slight bow. He sits back down and watches Nina, walking back to the complex unsteadily through the dune park. He listens to the murmur of the sea and feels tears rise again, tears of anger and sadness. He sees his Felice. But remotely now, not within his reach, as she was in the past months. He tries to repress her image.

He sees her stagger into the sea.

She looks back at him one last time.

Epilogue

The whole house is full of candles, very hard to come by and quite expensive. Especially the scented candles that spread a soft bouquet of lavender, jasmine and buttercups throughout the house. Max has been busy all day preparing a meal. A consommé with fresh herbs, ravioli with goat cheese and spinach and, for the main course, lasagna with aubergine, cultured meat and peeled tomato. The ice cream machine is already running to make creamy chocolate ice cream.

His house has been tidied and cleaned, he has taken a shower, shaved, brushed his teeth, cut his nails, washed his hair and he's wearing a nice, clean shirt.

The bottle of wine already open, he enjoys the first glass. A white wine from Mallorca. That too is special because you're supposed to eat and drink local products. Things that come from afar are exclusive and very expensive and a waste of energy.

When Eve comes in, she looks around interestedly; it's the first time she has visited him.

It looks very cosy, she says. She sniffs the air, tries to guess what the scent is, can only identify the lavender. After a cursory inspection of the living room and the view from the balcony, she sits down at the dining table. He pours her wine and raises his half-empty glass.

We toast to my recovered health, he says solemnly.

Really? And who declared you healthy? She chuckles as she says that.

I did. Surely that's the way it should be in any good therapy? I'm the only one who can declare it.

Eve smiles at him sweetly. She sips her wine and straightens the cutlery. Max serves the consommé and they both slurp from the hot liquid. Eve says she's never had such a delicious broth. They chat a bit about broth and how to make it. He looks at how she eats again, which he finds so erotic, her slightly nervous attitude when she looks at him or when she says something in her warm voice. In the candlelight and surrounded by all the scents, he finds her more beautiful than ever.

For days he had stared out of the window. He didn't want to see anyone. Only Aïcha came by every day to bring him some food. He couldn't get the image of Felice drowning in the waters of the Persian Gulf out of his head. Anger, helplessness and that strange feeling that it had happened almost a hundred years ago meant that he couldn't stop himself from thinking about it, it kept going around his head day and night.

Aïcha kept talking to him every time she visited. At first very gently, later with more firmness. He had already known Felice was dead, hadn't he? That it couldn't have been a pretty death? He had nothing to blame himself for. And finally, Aïcha said something that did manage to snap him out of his gloomy mood.

If Felice saw you sitting here like this, she would really be turned off by you, she said.

After Max has cleared the plates of the main course, he puts a small velvet-lined box on the table in front of Eve. In his day, the contents would've been easy to guess, but Eve looks at it in amazement. She flips it open and exclaims in surprise: a ring?

Yes, a ring, says Max and he kneels down at her feet.

I don't really wear jewellery, says Eve. And why are you on your knees?

Come on, this is a ring with a purpose. Really?

Yes, really. Will you marry me?

Oh, no. That's very old-fashioned, Max. Getting married is what you do at the notary and they only need signatures, not rings. It's a formality.

Not to me. Max looks a little crestfallen and hesitates on whether or not to get up again. But then he says: a formality? You have all gone mad. I've finished my search for Felice and I have a new mission: to marry you, make you happy and to bring romance back to the Peoples' Union, starting here with you. A proposal on my knees, a vow, a ring, big party, flinging bouquets, the whole shebang.

Eve laughs. It's a laugh somewhere between laughing out loud and laughing with pity.

If we live in a vulvocracy now, that can't have been abolished, can it? continues Max. Women used to love that stuff. And isn't it wonderful when you promise each other to stay together until death do you part?

Well, says Eve. Okay, then. A party sounds like fun. But there's really no need for that ring, though. Just get up now, will you?

THE END

What it takes to live in harmony with nature and each other in 2125 is explored in the non-fiction book **The Only Possible Solution** *(out January 21, 2026).*
Join the debate 'Shape the future' at 2125.world.

Printed in Dunstable, United Kingdom